D0573696

BOOKS BY JONATHAN KELLERMAN

FICTION

ALEX DELAWARE NOVELS

Breakdown (2016)

Motive (2015)

Killer (2014)

Guilt (2013)

Victims (2012)

Mystery (2011)

Deception (2010)

Evidence (2009)

Bones (2008)

Compulsion (2008)

Obsession (2007)

Gone (2006)

Rage (2005)

Therapy (2004)

A Cold Heart (2003)

The Murder Book (2002)

Flesh and Blood (2001)

Dr. Death (2000)

Monster (1999)

Survival of the Fittest (1997)

The Clinic (1997)

The Web (1996)

Self-Defense (1995)

Bad Love (1994)

Devil's Waltz (1993)

Private Eyes (1992)

Time Bomb (1990)

Silent Partner (1989)

Over the Edge (1987)

Blood Test (1986)

When the Bough Breaks (1985)

OTHER NOVELS

The Murderer's Daughter (2015)

The Golem of Paris (with Jesse Kellerman, 2015)

The Golem of Hollywood (with Jesse Kellerman, 2014)

True Detectives (2009)

Capital Crimes (with Faye Kellerman, 2006)

Twisted (2004)

Double Homicide (with Faye Kellerman, 2004)

The Conspiracy Club (2003)

Billy Straight (1998)

The Butcher's Theater (1988)

GRAPHIC NOVELS

Monster (2017)

The Web (2014)

Silent Partner (2012)

NONFICTION

With Strings Attached: The Art and Beauty of Vintage Guitars (2008)

Savage Spawn: Reflections on Violent Children (1999)

Helping the Fearful Child (1981)

Psychological Aspects of Childhood Cancer (1980)

FOR CHILDREN, WRITTEN AND ILLUSTRATED

Jonathan Kellerman's ABC of Weird Creatures (1995)

Daddy, Daddy, Can You Touch the Sky? (1994)

MONSTER

MONSTER

THE GRAPHIC NOVEL

JONATHAN KELLERMAN

ADAPTED BY **ANDE PARKS**
ART BY **MICHAEL GAYDOS**

BALLANTINE BOOKS • **NEW YORK**

Monster: The Graphic Novel is a work of fiction. Names, characters, places, and incidents are the products of the author's imagination or are used fictitiously. Any resemblance to actual events, locales, or persons, living or dead, is entirely coincidental.

Published in the United States by Ballantine Books, an imprint of Random House, a division of Penguin Random House LLC, New York.

Ballantine Books and the House colophon are registered trademarks of Penguin Random House LLC.

Hardback ISBN 978-0-345-54151-2
Ebook ISBN 978-0-345-54152-9

Printed in the United States of America on acid-free paper

randomhousebooks.com

9 8 7 6 5 4 3 2 1

First Edition

Text design by Dana Hayward

MONSTER

THE GIANT KNEW RICHARD NIXON.

SECRET SERVICE. **VICTORIA'S** SECRET SERVICE IN THE CLOSET UNDERWEAR UNDER-COVER.

LOOKIN' OUT FOR THE GUY GOOD OLD NIXON RMN **RIMMIN,** CUTTIN' OUTTA THE WHITE HOUSE NIGHT HOUSE DOING THE PARTY THING **ALL** HOURS WITH KURT VONNEGUT J. D. SALINGER.

GOT SHOT PROTECTING OLD RIMMIN. HE DIED ANYWAY...POOR OLD RICHARD NO **ALMANAC...**

HE REVEALED SCARRED FLESH. AN ORGANIC PEG LEG.

...I COULDN'T **STOP** IT.

HE SMELLED OF VINEGAR. HE WAS ALMOST BROAD ENOUGH TO SHADE BOTH MILO AND ME.

WE COULD HAVE USED A BREAK FROM THE SUN. I WAS **COOKING** IN MY SUIT. MILO'S SPORT COAT WAS SOAKED AT THE ARMPITS.

THE GIANT'S GRIZZLED SKIN WAS **DRY** AS BONE.

CHET...

I SOLD CAT'S CRADLE TO VONNEGUT FOR TEN BUCKS. BILLY BATHGATE TYPED THE—

YOU SHOULD MAKE IT TO THE TV ROOM TODAY. GONNA SHOW A PATRIOTIC MOVIE.

MAYBE SING "THE STAR-SPANGLED BANNER." WE COULD USE YOUR VOICE.

YEAH, PAVAROTTI. HE AND DOMINGO WERE AT CAESAR'S PALACE THEY DIDN'T LIKE THE—

WET. HE'S WET.

DON'T WORRY ABOUT IT, CHET. YOU KNOW SHARBNO AND HIS BLADDER. WE'LL HANDLE IT.

THIS WAY, GENTLEMEN.

GUY THAT SIZE, HOW CAN YOU *CONTROL* HIM?

WE DON'T. CLOZAPINE DOES.

LAST MONTH HIS DOSAGE GOT *UPPED* AFTER HE BEAT UP ANOTHER PATIENT. BROKE ABOUT A DOZEN BONES.

HEH...HE'S ON FOURTEEN HUNDRED MILLIGRAMS NOW. PRETTY *THOROUGH*, WOULDN'T YOU SAY, DOCTOR?

MAXIMUM'S *USUALLY* AROUND NINE HUNDRED. MOST DO WELL ON A THIRD OF THAT.

WE WALKED PAST A DOZEN INMATES. EMPTY EYES, STAINED KHAKI UNIFORMS.

WHAT GOT CHET IN HERE?

OUR GUIDE, AN ADMINISTRATOR NAMED FRANK DOLLARD, LED US THROUGH THE YARD, TAKING LONG, CALM STRIDES.

SAME AS ALL OF THEM. INCOMPETENT TO STAND TRIAL. YOUR BASIC 1026.

CHET WAS LIVING ON A MOUNTAIN DOWN SOUTH. A COUPLE OF HIKERS JUST HAPPENED TO PICK THE *WRONG* CAVE TO CAMP IN.

CHET WENT AT 'EM WITH HIS BARE HANDS. TORE THEM APART. RIPPED THE GIRL'S ARMS OFF.

HE WAS JUST SITTING THERE NEXT TO THE BODIES WHEN THEY FOUND HIM, LOOKING SCARED SOMEONE WAS GONNA HIT HIM. SOME SHERIFF SHOT-GUNNED HIS LEG CHARGING IN.

AUTHORIZED PERSONNEL

GATE G

AT THIS POINT HE JUST BEATS PEOPLE UP EVERY NOW AND THEN. **PROGRESS.**

I **KNOW** WHAT YOU'RE THINKING, DETECTIVE STURGIS: WE MIGHT AS WELL HAUL HIM OUT AND **SHOOT** HIM. GOOD RIDDANCE.

COP THINKING. I USED TO BE ON THE JOB, WOULDA SAID THE **SAME** THING. A COUPLE OF YEARS HERE AT STARKWEATHER, AND NOW I **KNOW** BETTER.

THESE GUYS COULDN'T **HELP** THEMSELVES ANY MORE THAN A BABY CRAPPING ITS DIAPER.

THEIR WIRING'S SCREWY.

SOME PEOPLE JUST TURN TO GARBAGE, AND THIS IS THE DUMPSTER.

EXACTLY WHY WE'RE HERE.

I DON'T KNOW ABOUT THAT. DR. ARGENT WORKED HERE, BUT SHE GOT KILLED OUT THERE... IN THE **CIVILIZED** WORLD.

AND THE WAY YOU **FOUND** HER, IN THAT CAR TRUNK, ALL CLEANED UP? TOO **NEAT** FOR OUR GUYS. TOO **PLANNED.**

GATE **G**

ONLY SECURITY I.D. REQUIRED

TICE

I'M NOT SAYING OUR GUYS ARE **HARMLESS,** EVEN WITH ALL THE DOPE WE PUMP INTO THEM, BUT THEY DON'T KILL FOR FUN.

THEY DON'T TAKE MUCH **PLEASURE** FROM LIFE, PERIOD, IF YOU CAN EVEN CALL WHAT THEY'RE DOING LIVING.

ICE

"MAKES YOU WONDER WHY GOD WOULD TAKE THE TROUBLE TO CREATE SUCH A **MESS** IN THE FIRST PLACE."

NINETEEN HOURS EARLIER.

TWO **CORPSES** IN TWO CAR TRUNKS. A WANNA-BE ACTOR NAMED RICHARD DADA AND, EIGHT MONTHS LATER, CLAIRE ARGENT, A PSYCHOLOGIST AT STARKWEATHER.

AS THE ONLY OPENLY GAY DETECTIVE ON THE FORCE, MILO WOULD ALWAYS BE AN OUTSIDER.

HIS CLEAR RATE—THE HIGHEST ON THE FORCE—PROVIDED JOB INSURANCE.

BUT HE'D MADE **ZERO** PROGRESS ON THESE TWO CASES, AND IT RUBBED HIS NERVES **RAW**.

THEY DESERVE **MORE**, ALEX.

DADA WAS JUST ANOTHER DUMB KID WHO COMES OUT HERE, LOOKING TO BE RICH AND FAMOUS. ENDS UP SLICED IN **HALF**, WITH HIS DAMN **EYES** CUT OUT.

NOW DR. ARGENT, KILLED THE SAME WAY, 'CEPT HER EYES WERE JUST CHOPPED UP LIKE HAMBURGER.

WAS SHE CUT IN HALF?

NO, BUT WRAPPED IN TWO GARBAGE BAGS, LIKE DADA. MY THEORY IS THERE WAS NO NEED TO BREAK OUT THE SAW.

DADA WAS **TALL** AND DROVE A VW. ARGENT FIT INTO HER BUICK, NO PROBLEM.

5

I KNOW WE'VE COVERED IT **BEFORE**, BUT LET'S GO BACK TO DADA.

ALL RIGHT. CORONER SAYS THE THROAT WOUND KILLED HIM. THE MUTILATION CAME AFTER.

HE WAS SLICED STRAIGHT THROUGH, PROBABLY WITH A BAND SAW.

SOMEONE SECTIONED THE KID LIKE A SLAB OF BEEF.

NO FORENSIC EVIDENCE?

NOPE. NO FOREIGN HAIRS OR FLUIDS. I GOT THE CASE IN THE FIRST PLACE BECAUSE THE LIEUTENANT ASSUMED DADA WAS GAY.

THE MUTILATION... WHEN HOMOSEXUALS FREAK, THEY GO ALL THE WAY, BLAH BLAH BLAH.

HORSESHIT. DADA HAD NO TIES TO THE GAY COMMUNITY, AND HIS PARENTS SAID HE ALWAYS HAD GIRLFRIENDS BACK HOME.

WOMEN? NOT THAT I'VE FOUND. HE LIVED IN A LITTLE STUDIO PLACE NEAR LA BREA AND SUNSET. TINY, BUT HE KEPT IT NEAT.

WHAT ABOUT **HERE**?

THAT CAN BE A **DICEY** NEIGHBOR-HOOD.

YEAH, BUT THE BUILDING HAD A KEY CARD PARKING LOT AND SECURITY CAMERAS.

THE KID WAS **CLEAN**, ALEX.

HELL, I DON'T KNOW. MAYBE HE JUST RAN INTO THE **WRONG** PSYCHOPATH.

THE FBI SAYS EYE MUTILATION IMPLIES MORE THAN A *CAUSAL* RELATIONSHIP.

I SENT THEM THE CRIME-SCENE DATA QUESTIONNAIRE, GOT BACK DOUBLE-TALK ABOUT KNOWN ASSOCIATES. PROBLEM IS, I CAN'T FIND ANY. HE'D ONLY BEEN OUT HERE NINE MONTHS.

NOT MUCH TIME, BUT MAYBE HE MADE SOME *SHOWBIZ* CONNECTIONS.

IF SO, IT WASN'T AT A *STUDIO.* I FOUND A WANT AD FROM THE WEEKLY IN ONE OF HIS JACKETS. TINY PRINT THING, OPEN CASTING CALL FOR SOME FLICK CALLED *BLOOD WALK.*

THERE'S A COPY IN THERE SOMEWHERE.

I TRIED TO TRACE THE NUMBER. IT BELONGED TO SOME OUTFIT CALLED THIN LINE PRODUCTIONS. LONG GONE NOW, AND I CAN'T FIND ANYONE WHO'S HEARD OF THEM.

BLOOD WALK.
Thin Line Productions
Hollywood-555 877 9981

BLOOD WALK.

YEAH, I *KNOW,* BUT I'VE TAKEN IT AS FAR AS I CAN.

SO... CLAIRE ARGENT?

THIRTY-NINE-YEARS-OLD, DIVORCED, LIVED ALONE. OH, AND SHE WAS A *PSYCHOLOGIST.* I DON'T SUPPOSE YOU KNEW HER?

NO.

HOME ADDRESS IN THE HOLLYWOOD HILLS, BUT SHE WAS FOUND IN WEST L.A. SO FAR, I'VE GOT *ABOUT* AS MUCH AS I HAVE ON DADA.

NOTHING TO TIE THEM *TOGETHER* EXCEPT A LACK OF "KNOWN ASSOCIATES," AND THE WAY THEY *DIED.*

I'M HEADED TO HER WORKPLACE TOMORROW... THOUGHT YOU MIGHT LIKE TO TAG ALONG.

STARKWEATHER HOSPITAL: GHOUL CENTRAL. EVER BEEN THERE?

NO. NO REASON...

"...NONE OF MY PATIENTS EVER KILLED ANYONE."

WE ARRIVED THE NEXT AFTERNOON. STARKWEATHER HOME FOR THE CRIMINALLY INSANE. IN POLITICAL JARGON, A "MAJOR MENTAL HYGIENE FACILITY."

IN *REALITY,* SECURE HOUSING FOR SPREE MURDERERS, CANNIBALS, SODOMIZERS, CHILD-RAPERS AND CHANTING ZOMBIES. *ANYONE* TOO CRAZY AND DANGEROUS FOR SAN QUENTIN OR PELICAN BAY.

STARKWEATHER STATE HOSPITAL FOR THE CRIMINALLY INSANE

FIVE STORIES OF CEMENT BLOCK AND GRAY STUCCO. PUNITIVELY UGLY.

GENTLEMEN. I'M BILL SWIG, THE SUPERINTENDENT HERE AT STARK-WEATHER.

THANKS FOR ESCORTING OUR GUESTS IN, FRANK.

PLEASE, SIT. SORRY TO KEEP YOU WAITING. TRAGEDY, DR. ARGENT. I'M STILL SHOCKED.

SO, ANY IDEAS ABOUT HER MURDER?

I CAN UNDER-STAND YOUR THINKING IT MIGHT BE WORK-RELATED, BUT I TERM THAT IMPOSSIBLE.

DR. ARGENT'S PATIENTS ARE HERE, AND SHE WAS MURDERED OUT THERE.

ADD TO THAT THE FACT THAT HER TENURE WAS **TROUBLE-FREE**. SHE RAN A LIFE SKILLS GROUP FOR SOME OF THE MEN. I BELIEVE A TECH NAMED HEIDI OTT HELPED WITH THAT.

EVERYONE LIKED CLAIRE, PATIENTS INCLUDED.

THAT MAKES THE PATIENTS SEEM **RATIONAL**, AND I THOUGHT THE MEN HERE WERE ANYTHING BUT. WHAT'S TO SAY ONE OF THEM DIDN'T HEAR A VOICE TELLING HIM TO CUT DR. ARGENT'S THROAT?

YES. WELL, THEY **ARE** PSYCHOTIC, BUT MOST OF THEM ARE VERY WELL-MAINTAINED, AS I'M **SURE** FRANK TOLD YOU.

BUT WHAT'S THE **DIFFERENCE**? THAT MAIN POINT IS, THEY DON'T **LEAVE** HERE.

PULLING OUT THE NOTEPAD **ALWAYS** GOT A REACTION. SWIG RAISED HIS EYEBROWS.

NO ONE **EVER** GETS OUT?

VERY, **VERY** RARELY. ONLY TWO PERCENT EVER TRY TO ATTAIN **RELEASE**. THE FEW THAT MAKE IT PAST OUR REVIEW COMMITTEE ARE PLACED IN WELL-SUPERVISED FACILITIES.

BEFORE I ARRIVED FIVE YEARS AGO, THERE WERE A **FEW** PROBLEMS, BUT REALLY, IT'S A NON-ISSUE.

LOOK, DETECTIVE, I'M REALLY DON'T **GET** THIS LINE OF QUESTIONING. I DARE SAY, STARKWEATHER IS **SAFER** THAN THE TERRITORY ON YOUR BEAT.

OKAY, LET'S MOVE ON. WHAT CAN YOU TELL ME ABOUT DR. ARGENT'S PERSONALITY?

SHE WAS COMPETENT, **QUIET**. NO CONFLICTS. PATIENT RECORDS WOULD REQUIRE A COURT ORDER, BUT THIS MUCH I **CAN** GIVE YOU. CLAIRE'S PERSONNEL FILE.

THANK YOU.

LOOKING AT CLAIRE ARGENT'S HEADSHOT IN THE FILE, THE FIRST WORD TO COME TO MIND WAS "WHOLESOME." SHE LOOKED CLOSER TO THIRTY THAN THE THIRTY-NINE ESTABLISHED BY HER BIRTHDATE.

THE EYES WERE LUSTROUS, WARM... HER BEST FEATURE. NOW MANGLED. SOMEONE'S TROPHY?

AS I STARED AT HER, SWIG ASKED ABOUT MY EXPERIENCE WITH DANGEROUS PSYCHOTICS.

I'M A CLINICAL PSYCHOLOGIST. I DO OCCASIONAL CONSULTING WITH THE POLICE.

I ROTATED THROUGH ATASCADERO AS AN INTERN, BUT THAT'S ABOUT IT.

AH...BEFORE US, THAT WAS THE **TOUGHEST** PLACE. NOW WE GET THE WORST CASES, ALONG WITH THE 1368's: MALINGERING CRIMINALS WHO THINK THEY CAN FOOL THE SYSTEM.

THEY DROOL A BIT, THINKING THEY CAN AVOID SAN QUENTIN. WE EVALUATE THEM AND SEND THEM BACK.

THOSE CASES ARE HOUSED ON THE FIFTH FLOOR, TO MINIMIZE THE **DISTRACTION** THEY POSE TO OUR REAL **MISSION**: TREATING INSANE MURDERERS AND KEEPING THEM **INVISIBLE** TO THE WORLD.

IT'S LIKE SAUSAGE MAKING...THE **LESS** THE PUBLIC KNOWS ABOUT WHAT WE DO, THE **BETTER**. THAT'S WHY I HOPE CLAIRE'S MURDER DOESN'T PUT US IN THE SPOTLIGHT.

NOW THEN, I SUPPOSE YOU'D LIKE TO SEE HOW WE **DO** THINGS AROUND HERE BEFORE YOU GO.

PLEASED TO MEET YOU. I'M PHIL.

SWIG ARRANGED A TOUR GUIDE. PHIL HATTERSON'S EYES WERE HAZEL, ALERT, BUT SOFT... LIKE THOSE OF A TAME DEER.

HE WORE THE KHAKI UNIFORM OF AN INMATE.

TWO MINUTES AND ONE ELEVATOR RIDE LATER, WE WERE ON THE SECOND FLOOR, HOME TO THE BULK OF STARKWEATHER'S INMATES.

MED LINE FORM HERE NO PUSHING

IT COULD HAVE BEEN ANY HOSPITAL WARD, ASIDE FROM THE NURSING STATION COMPLETELY ENCASED IN PLASTIC. I TRIED TO LOOK AROUND WITHOUT BEING CONSPICUOUS.

MEN OF ALL COLORS, AGES AND SIZES. SOME WERE GAPE-JAWED CATATONIC. SOME WERE MUTTERING APPARITIONS NOT MUCH DIFFERENT FROM ANY WESTSIDE PANHANDLER. SOME, LIKE HATTERSON, LOOKED RELATIVELY NORMAL.

EVERY ONE OF THEM HAD DESTROYED HUMAN LIFE.

IN THE DISTANCE, SOMEONE CRIED OUT. SOMEONE ELSE LAUGHED.

THE AIR WAS FRIGID. OBVIOUSLY HEAVILY AIR-CONDITIONED, BUT SOMEHOW STILL STALE.

WE PASSED THE INMATES, ENDURING A PSYCHOTIC GAUNTLET. PHIL PAID NO NOTICE TO THE STARES AS HE DANCE-STEPPED US THROUGH.

A COUPLE OF MEN ARGUED LOUDLY, OBLIVIOUS TO OUR INTRUSION.

ANOTHER STARED AT US AS WE PASSED, HIS HAND MOVING FURIOUSLY IN HIS PANTS.

YOU LOST?

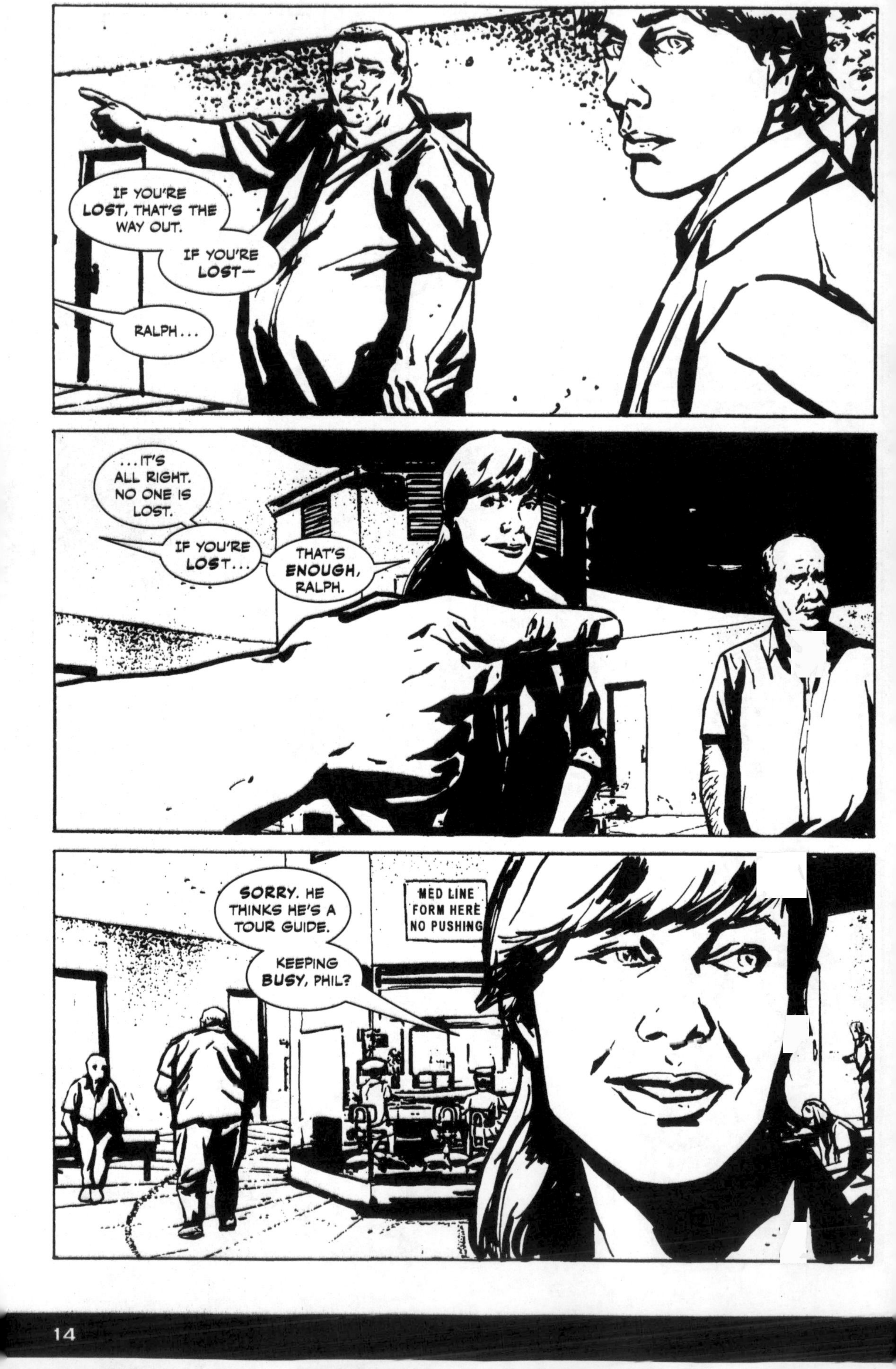
IF YOU'RE LOST, THAT'S THE WAY OUT.
IF YOU'RE LOST—
RALPH . . .
. . . IT'S ALL RIGHT. NO ONE IS LOST.
IF YOU'RE LOST . . .
THAT'S ENOUGH, RALPH.
SORRY. HE THINKS HE'S A TOUR GUIDE.
MED LINE FORM HERE NO PUSHING
KEEPING BUSY, PHIL?

I'M GIVING THEM A TOUR, MISS OTT.

THIS IS DETECTIVE STURGIS FROM THE LAPD, AND THIS IS DOCTOR... I'M SORRY.

DELAWARE.

HEIDI OTT. PLEASED TO MEET YOU.

THE THING ABOUT RALPH IS, HE USED TO CRUISE THE FREEWAYS, PICK PEOPLE UP HAVING CAR TROUBLE, THEN HE'D—

PHIL, WE RESPECT EACH OTHER'S PRIVACY, REMEMBER?

SORRY.

MED FORM HE NO PUSHING

YOU'RE HERE ABOUT DR. ARGENT?

YES, MA'AM. YOU WORKED WITH HER?

I WORKED WITH A GROUP SHE RAN. WE HAD CONTACT ABOUT SEVERAL OTHER PATIENTS.

WHEN YOU HAVE A CHANCE, I'D LIKE TO—

SHOUTING FROM JUST DOWN THE CORRIDOR INTERRUPTED MILO.

THE ARGUING MEN WERE ON THE FLOOR. A DOUBLE DERVISH OF CLAWING AND BITING, LIKE A PAIR OF WILD DOGS.

MED LINE FORM HERE NO PUSHING

OTT TOOK CHARGE QUICKLY, MOVING TOWARD THE FIGHT AND SUMMONING HELP.

IT WAS OVER IN LESS THAN A MINUTE, WITH MINIMAL DAMAGE DONE TO EITHER OF THE COMBATANTS.

MED LINE FORM HERE NO PUSHING

I HATE WHEN STUPID STUFF HAPPENS. WHAT'S THE POINT?

WELL, SHALL WE CONTINUE?

THE TOUR CONTINUED. A TV ROOM, A SMALL COMMON ROOM THAT SERVED AS A LIBRARY...

...AND ONE OF THE FOUR-INMATE LIVING QUARTERS.

PHIL, DID YOU **KNOW** DR. ARGENT?

SURE, OF COURSE. VERY NICE LADY. I MEAN, SHE SEEMED VERY SMART. SHE WAS...**NICE.**

DO YOU KNOW WHAT **HAPPENED** TO HER?

OH, SURE. **EVERYONE** DOES. THEY LET US READ THE PAPER. WE CAN READ ANYTHING.

AND, OF COURSE, WE GET OUR **MEALS.** THREE SQUARES A DAY. FOOD'S PRETTY TASTY, TOO.

CHAPTER PRESIDENT OF THE STARKWEATHER CHAMBER OF COMMERCE. I COULD SEE WHY SWIG HAD PICKED HIM.

THE TOUR CONTINUED. WE WALKED THROUGH THE UPPER WARDS QUICKLY. NO FIGHTS, NOTHING UNTOWARD.

THE SAME MIX OF DEGRADED MUSCLES, STUPOR AND SELF-ABSORPTION, OCCASIONAL DARK STARES RIFE WITH PARANOIA.

HATTERSON MOVED US THROUGH QUICKLY, NO MORE HAPPY CHATTER. HE SEEMED DEFEATED, ALMOST PEEVISH.

WITH HIS CHATTER GONE, THE CORRIDORS WERE STRIPPED OF CONVERSATION. NO DISCOURSE AMONG THE INMATES.

HERE, EVERY MAN WAS AN ISLAND.

I THOUGHT ABOUT HOW HEIDI OTT HAD BEEN ABLE TO BREAK UP THE FIGHT SO QUICKLY. IN A PRISON, A SKIRMISH LIKE THAT COULD HAVE LED TO A FULL-SCALE RIOT.

MEDICATION PLAYED A LARGE PART, BUT STARKWEATHER DID *SEEM* TO BE A TIGHT SHIP. FULL OF ONE-WAY PASSENGERS, MEANING THE CHANCE THAT CLAIRE ARGENT'S WORK HAD ANYTHING TO DO WITH HER MURDER WAS REMOTE.

BUT HAD THE SYSTEM **BROKEN** DOWN SOMEHOW? A RELEASED MAN "ACTING OUT" IN THE WORST WAY?

MAYBE **HEIDI** COULD TELL US. SHE'D WORKED WITH CLAIRE ARGENT ON THE LIVING SKILLS GROUP. **WHAT** HAD CLAIRE HAD IN MIND WHEN SETTING UP THE SESSIONS?

WHY HAD SHE COME HERE?

THANKS FOR THE TOUR, PHIL.

SO... HOW LONG HAVE YOU BEEN HERE?

A LONG TIME.

WHAT'S THAT, PHIL?

A LONG TIME.

GODDAMN WEENIE.

DIDN'T REALLY GET TO SPEAK WITH THE OTT GIRL. I'LL HAVE TO FOLLOW UP.

SO... EVERYONE HERE SPOUTS THE SAME LINE: "THIS PLACE IS AS SAFE AS MILK." YOU BUY IT?

THEY BROKE UP THAT FIGHT PRETTY FAST.

FRANK DOLLARD APPROACHED, CUTTING OFF OUR SPECULATIONS.

WELL, LOOK HERE. ONE TOUR GUIDE DEPARTS, AND ANOTHER ARRIVES. DON'T WANT US WANDERING AROUND ON OUR OWN, DO THEY?

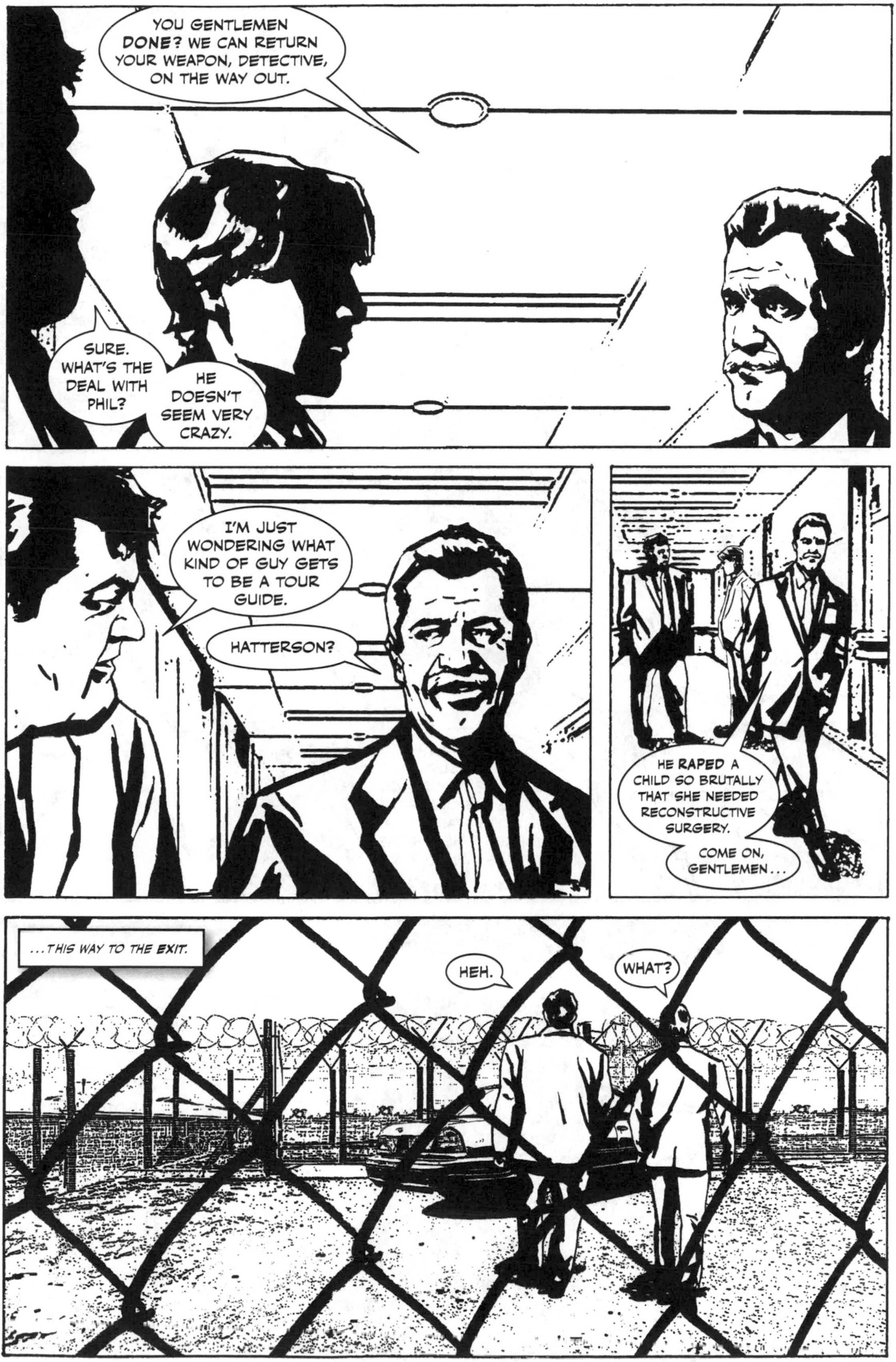
YOU GENTLEMEN DONE? WE CAN RETURN YOUR WEAPON, DETECTIVE, ON THE WAY OUT.
SURE. WHAT'S THE DEAL WITH PHIL?
HE DOESN'T SEEM VERY CRAZY.
I'M JUST WONDERING WHAT KIND OF GUY GETS TO BE A TOUR GUIDE.
HATTERSON?
HE RAPED A CHILD SO BRUTALLY THAT SHE NEEDED RECONSTRUCTIVE SURGERY.
COME ON, GENTLEMEN...
...THIS WAY TO THE EXIT.
HEH.
WHAT?

HOW'S **THIS** FOR A STORY LINE: WE CATCH THE BAD GUY. TURNS OUT HE IS SOME JOKER THEY LET OUT BY MISTAKE. HE PLEADS **INSANITY,** ENDS UP **RIGHT** BACK HERE.

SELL IT TO HOLLYWOOD. NO... NOT STUPID ENOUGH.

THEN **AGAIN,** YOU TELL ME OUR BOY PROBABLY DOESN'T LOOK OR ACT CRAZY. MAYBE I SHOULD **FORGET** ABOUT THIS PLACE.

MY GUESS IS OUR GUY IS MORE LIKE A FIFTH-FLOOR RESIDENT. A **PRETENDER** IN A PLACE LIKE THIS.

WHAT'S WITH THAT GROUP OF CLAIRE'S? WHY **TEACH** THOSE GUYS LIFE SKILLS. HELL, WHY WAS SHE AT STARKWEATHER IN THE **FIRST** PLACE?

WHY LEAVE HER CAREER AT COUNTY GENERAL FOR THIS? I **WONDERED,** TOO.

MAYBE THE **STRUCTURE?** NO MORE APPLYING FOR GRANTS AND PLAYING THE ACADEMIC GAMES?

WELL, I GOTTA GO BACK TO **BASIC** DETECTIVE DOGMA: LAY YOUR **FOUNDATION.** GET TO KNOW THE VIC. I FEEL THE SAME ABOUT ARGENT AND DADA, THOUGH... GRABBING AIR.

BOTH INOFFENSIVE, SEEM-INGLY **LONELY** PEOPLE. SPEAKING OF...

"...LET ME SHOW YOU HER HOUSE."

ONE OF THE COUNTLESS UNADORNED, LATE-FIFTIES KNOCKUPS POSING AS INTENTIONALLY CONTEMPORARY.

THE STREET, CAPE HORN DRIVE, WAS A SHORT, STRAIGHT AFTERTHOUGHT OF A SLIT INTO THE NORTH SIDE OF WOODROW WILSON.

COZY. YOU GUYS REMOVE ANYTHING?

THIS IS THE WAY WE FOUND IT. CLEAN. SIMPLE. LIKE DADA'S PAD.

FINGERPRINT POWDER EVERYWHERE. THE COPS HAD GONE THROUGH THE ENTIRE PLACE.

THE REST OF THE PLACE WAS AS BARREN AS THE LIVING ROOM. THE OFFICE, AT LEAST, HAD SOME FURNITURE: PLYWOOD SHELVES STUFFED WITH VOLUMES ON PSYCHOLOGY AND BOUND STACKS OF JOURNALS ARRANGED BY DATES.

I FOUND HER **DIVORCE** PAPERS IN THIS CARDBOARD BOX, NEAR THE TOP.

WHAT ELSE? OKAY... **HERE** WE GO.

CENTURY BANK BALANCE BOOK. SUNSET AND CAHUENGA.

WELL, WELL, WELL... LOOKS LIKE SHE WAS DOING **OKAY.**

SAVINGS ACCOUNT WITH A **BALANCE** OF $240,000 AND SOME CENTS. STEADY PATTERN... DEPOSITS OF THREE GRAND AT THE END OF EVERY MONTH.

NO WAY SHE MADE ENOUGH TO SET ASIDE THAT MUCH, EVEN **LIVING** LIKE THIS.

WE FLIPPED THROUGH OTHER PAPERWORK: CHECKING ACCOUNT BALANCES, TAX RETURNS, CREDIT CARD STATEMENTS. SHE SPENT LITTLE, AND SHE PAID EVERYTHING ON TIME.

I THOUGHT ABOUT WHAT WE **DIDN'T** FIND: MEMENTOS, PHOTOGRAPHS, CORRESPONDENCE. ANYTHING PERSONAL.

NO RECORD OF RENT CHECKS, BUT NO PROPERTY TAX RECEIPTS.

MAYBE THE EX PAID THE MORTGAGE AND TAXES. MAYBE THAT WAS HIS ALIMONY.

AND NOW THAT SHE'S GONE, HE'S OFF THE HOOK. AND IF HE'S MAINTAINED SOME OWNERSHIP OF THE HOUSE, THERE'S A BIT OF INCENTIVE FOR YOU.

ANY IDEA WHO GETS THE TWO HUNDRED FORTY? DID YOU FIND A WILL?

NOT YET. SO YOU LIKE THE HUSBAND?

I'M JUST THINKING ABOUT WHAT YOU ALWAYS TELL ME. FOLLOW THE MONEY.

HE GRUNTED. WE CONTINUED TO DIG.

JOURNALS. DR. CLAIRE ARGENT HAS AUTHORED A DOZEN STUDIES, ALL ALONG THE SAME LINES: THE EFFECTS OF ALCOHOL ON HUMAN MOTOR SKILLS.

THE RESULTS WERE CONSISTENT, IF SOMEWHAT DULL: BOOZE SLOWED YOU DOWN.

ONE INTERESTING FACT: SHE'D ALWAYS PUBLISHED SOLO. UNUSUAL IN ACADEMIC MEDICINE. GOING ALONE. AS ALWAYS, IT SEEMED.

SUCH A SPARE LIFE.
BLANK. *HOLLOW*. NULL.

AFTER FIVE *YEARS* WITH DRUNKS AND SIX MONTHS
WITH DANGEROUS PSYCHOTICS, MAYBE CLAIRE HAD
CRAVED SILENCE. *SIMPLICITY*. BUT THAT DIDN'T
EXPLAIN THE LACK OF LETTERS FROM HOME, NOT
EVEN A SNAPSHOT OF PARENTS, NIECES, NEPHEWS.
SOME KIND OF *CONTACT*.

I KEPT SEARCHING FOR *REASONS* SHE'D TRADED
COUNTY FOR STARKWEATHER. EVEN WITH COMPARABLE
SALARIES, A CIVIL SERVICE POSITION WAS A
COMEDOWN FROM THE WHITE-COAT WORK SHE'D
BEEN DOING. AND IF SHE'D CRAVED *CONTACT* WITH
SCHIZOPHRENICS, COUNTY HAD PLENTY OF THOSE.
DANGEROUS PATIENTS? THE JAIL WARD WAS RIGHT
THERE.

THERE HAD TO BE SOME *OTHER* REASON FOR WHAT I
COULDN'T STOP THINKING OF AS A SELF-DEMOTION.
IT WAS ALMOST AS IF SHE'D PUNISHED HERSELF. FOR
WHAT? OR HAD SHE BEEN FLEEING SOMETHING?

HAD IT CAUGHT UP WITH HER?

MILO DROPPED ME AT MY NEW HOUSE. THREE YEARS, AND I STILL THOUGHT OF IT AS A BIT OF AN INTERLOPER.

A PSYCHOPATH HAD TORCHED MY OLD HOME TO CINDERS. ROBIN HAD SUPERVISED THE CONSTRUCTION OF THIS VERSION: WHITE, OPEN AND AIRY. I TOLD HER I LOVED IT AND, FOR THE MOST PART, I DID.

ONE DAY, I'D STOP BEING SO SECRETLY STODGY.

THERE HE IS! HOW'D IT GO?

UNEVENTFUL.

MMM...THAT PLACE MADE YOU ROMANTIC?

BEING OUT OF THERE MAKES ME ROMANTIC. IT'S REALLY NOT DANGEROUS, ROBIN.

CHOCK FULL OF MURDERERS AND NO DANGER?

PEOPLE GO TO WORK THERE EVERY DAY AND NOTHING HAPPENS.

EVERYONE SEEMS TO THINK IT'S SAFER THAN THE STREETS.

MEANWHILE, THAT PSYCHOLOGIST GETS STUFFED IN A CAR TRUNK. ANYWAY, THE MAIN THING IS YOU'RE BACK. DINNER?

MAYBE.

MAYBE LATER.

I KNOW I'M **HARPING**, BUT NEXT TIME YOU GO TO THAT PLACE, PLEASE CALL THE MINUTE YOU GET OUT.

I WILL. YOU WERE **REALLY** WORRIED?

AX MURDERERS AND VAMPIRES. LORD **KNOWS** WHAT ELSE?

ROB, THE MEN I SAW TODAY WERE **SUBMISSIVE**.

EXCEPT FOR THE BEARDED FELLOW WHO'D CHARGED US IN THE YARD. THE FIGHT IN THE HALL. PLASTIC WINDOWS. PADDED ELEVATORS.

SO YOU LEARNED NOTHING THERE?

NOT REALLY. LATER WE WENT TO CLAIRE ARGENT'S HOUSE.

I DESCRIBED THE PLACE, THEN ASKED ROBIN WHAT SHE THOUGHT OF IT.

WOULD I WANT TO LIVE LIKE THAT? NOT **FOREVER**, BUT MAYBE FOR A SHORT STRETCH. NICE TO TAKE A BREAK FROM ALL THE COMPLICATIONS.

COMPLICATIONS?

NOT YOU, HONEY. JUST... **CIRCUMSTANCES**. OBLIGATIONS. DEADLINES... LIFE JUST PILING UP.

SOMETIMES A LITTLE **SIMPLICITY** DOESN'T SOUND BAD.

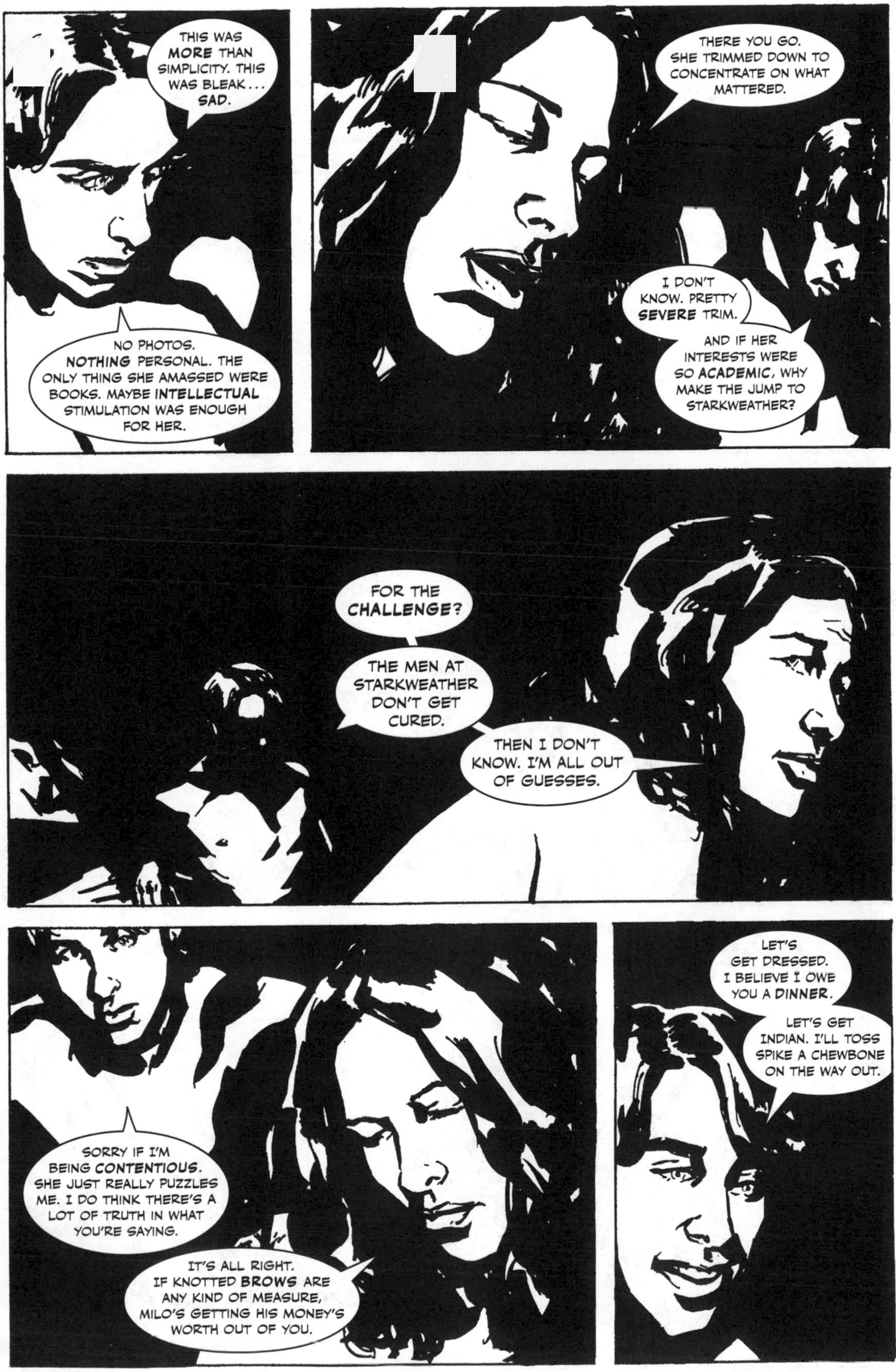
THIS WAS MORE THAN SIMPLICITY. THIS WAS BLEAK . . . SAD.
NO PHOTOS. NOTHING PERSONAL. THE ONLY THING SHE AMASSED WERE BOOKS. MAYBE INTELLECTUAL STIMULATION WAS ENOUGH FOR HER.
THERE YOU GO. SHE TRIMMED DOWN TO CONCENTRATE ON WHAT MATTERED.
I DON'T KNOW. PRETTY SEVERE TRIM.
AND IF HER INTERESTS WERE SO ACADEMIC, WHY MAKE THE JUMP TO STARKWEATHER?
FOR THE CHALLENGE?
THE MEN AT STARKWEATHER DON'T GET CURED.
THEN I DON'T KNOW. I'M ALL OUT OF GUESSES.
SORRY IF I'M BEING CONTENTIOUS. SHE JUST REALLY PUZZLES ME. I DO THINK THERE'S A LOT OF TRUTH IN WHAT YOU'RE SAYING.
IT'S ALL RIGHT. IF KNOTTED BROWS ARE ANY KIND OF MEASURE, MILO'S GETTING HIS MONEY'S WORTH OUT OF YOU.
LET'S GET DRESSED. I BELIEVE I OWE YOU A DINNER.
LET'S GET INDIAN. I'LL TOSS SPIKE A CHEWBONE ON THE WAY OUT.

MILO CALLED EARLY THE NEXT MORNING. I MET HIM BACK AT CLAIRE'S HOUSE AT 9:45. CLAIRE'S EX WAS TO BE THERE AT TEN.

DRIVING UP FROM SAN DIEGO? VERY *COOPERATIVE* FELLOW.

SAYS HE HAS *BUSINESS* UP HERE. HE'S A REAL ESTATE LAWYER, SO HE COMES UP HERE A LOT.

YEAH, I KNOW... I MADE NOTE OF THAT.

BY THE WAY, HE WASN'T AWARE OF ANY *WILL*. MY GUESS IS HER PARENTS WOULD BE FIRST IN LINE TO GET THE HOUSE. BUT, HE *IS* A LAWYER...

MAYBE HE GOT TIRED OF PAYING CLAIRE'S BILLS. IT COULD *CHAFE*, ESPECIALLY IF HE'S REMARRIED. OR MAYBE HE HAS MONEY TROUBLES.

WE'LL *SEE*. UNLESS I MISS MY GUESS, THIS BMW IS OUR MAN.

DETECTIVE MILO STURGIS. THANKS FOR COMING. THIS IS DR. DELAWARE, OUR PSYCHOLOGICAL CONSULTANT.

JOE STARGILL.

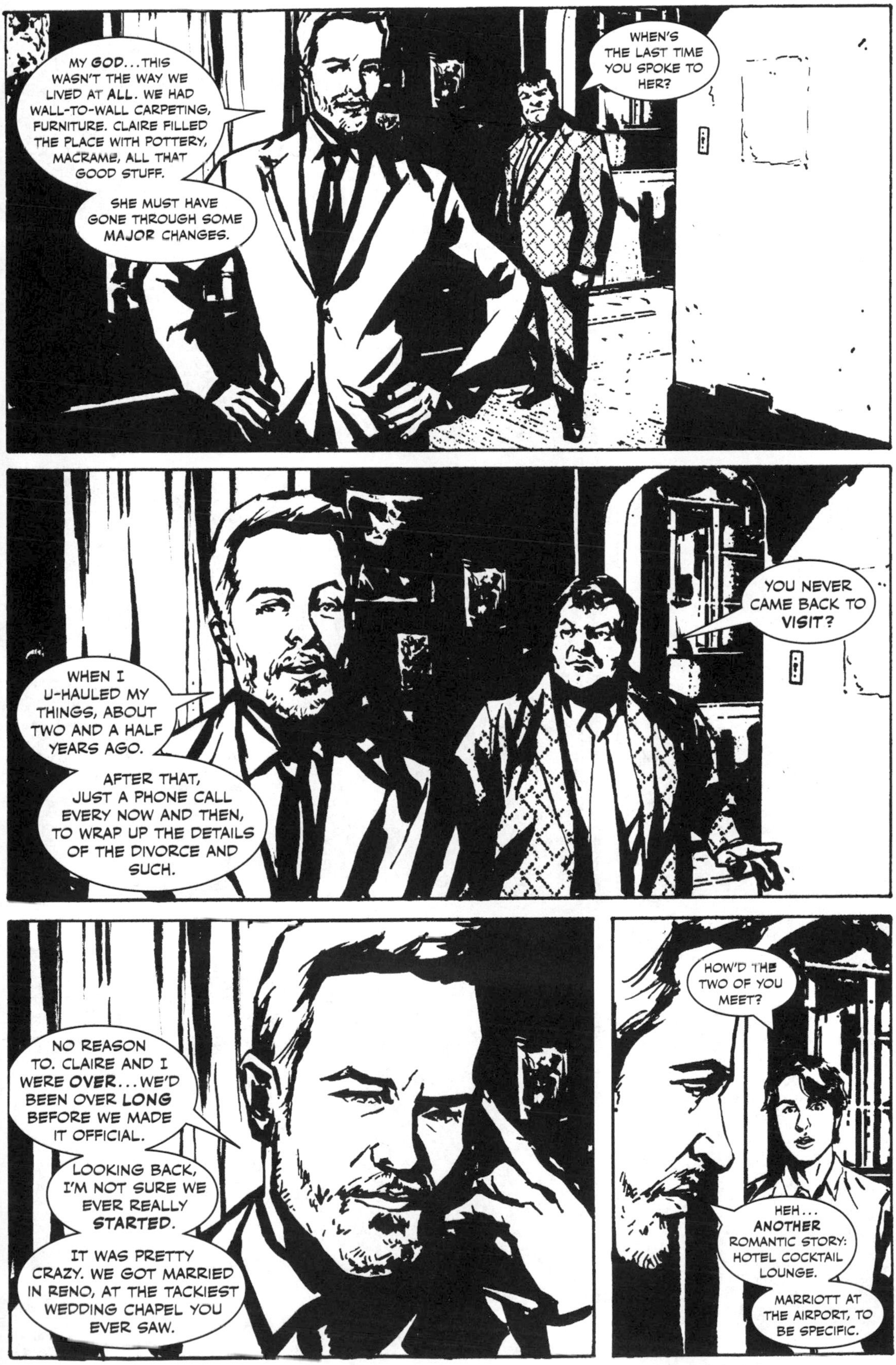
MY GOD... THIS WASN'T THE WAY WE LIVED AT ALL. WE HAD WALL-TO-WALL CARPETING, FURNITURE. CLAIRE FILLED THE PLACE WITH POTTERY, MACRAME, ALL THAT GOOD STUFF.
SHE MUST HAVE GONE THROUGH SOME MAJOR CHANGES.
WHEN'S THE LAST TIME YOU SPOKE TO HER?
WHEN I U-HAULED MY THINGS, ABOUT TWO AND A HALF YEARS AGO.
AFTER THAT, JUST A PHONE CALL EVERY NOW AND THEN, TO WRAP UP THE DETAILS OF THE DIVORCE AND SUCH.
YOU NEVER CAME BACK TO VISIT?
NO REASON TO. CLAIRE AND I WERE OVER... WE'D BEEN OVER LONG BEFORE WE MADE IT OFFICIAL.
LOOKING BACK, I'M NOT SURE WE EVER REALLY STARTED.
IT WAS PRETTY CRAZY. WE GOT MARRIED IN RENO, AT THE TACKIEST WEDDING CHAPEL YOU EVER SAW.
HOW'D THE TWO OF YOU MEET?
HEH... ANOTHER ROMANTIC STORY: HOTEL COCKTAIL LOUNGE.
MARRIOTT AT THE AIRPORT, TO BE SPECIFIC.

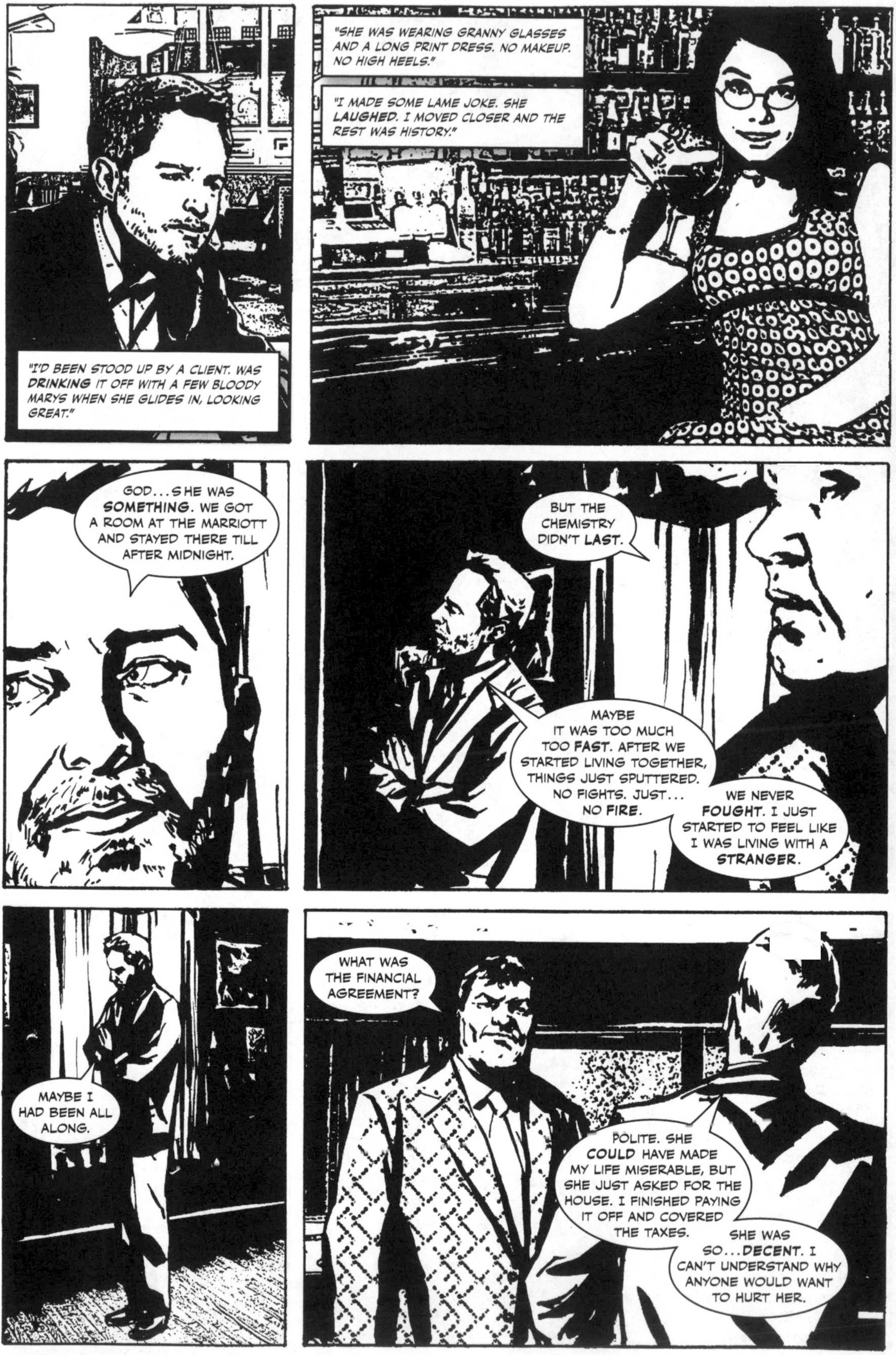
"I'D BEEN STOOD UP BY A CLIENT. WAS DRINKING IT OFF WITH A FEW BLOODY MARYS WHEN SHE GLIDES IN, LOOKING GREAT."
"SHE WAS WEARING GRANNY GLASSES AND A LONG PRINT DRESS. NO MAKEUP. NO HIGH HEELS."
"I MADE SOME LAME JOKE. SHE LAUGHED. I MOVED CLOSER AND THE REST WAS HISTORY."
GOD...SHE WAS SOMETHING. WE GOT A ROOM AT THE MARRIOTT AND STAYED THERE TILL AFTER MIDNIGHT.
BUT THE CHEMISTRY DIDN'T LAST.
MAYBE IT WAS TOO MUCH TOO FAST. AFTER WE STARTED LIVING TOGETHER, THINGS JUST SPUTTERED. NO FIGHTS. JUST... NO FIRE.
WE NEVER FOUGHT. I JUST STARTED TO FEEL LIKE I WAS LIVING WITH A STRANGER.
MAYBE I HAD BEEN ALL ALONG.
WHAT WAS THE FINANCIAL AGREEMENT?
POLITE. SHE COULD HAVE MADE MY LIFE MISERABLE, BUT SHE JUST ASKED FOR THE HOUSE. I FINISHED PAYING IT OFF AND COVERED THE TAXES.
SHE WAS SO...DECENT. I CAN'T UNDERSTAND WHY ANYONE WOULD WANT TO HURT HER.

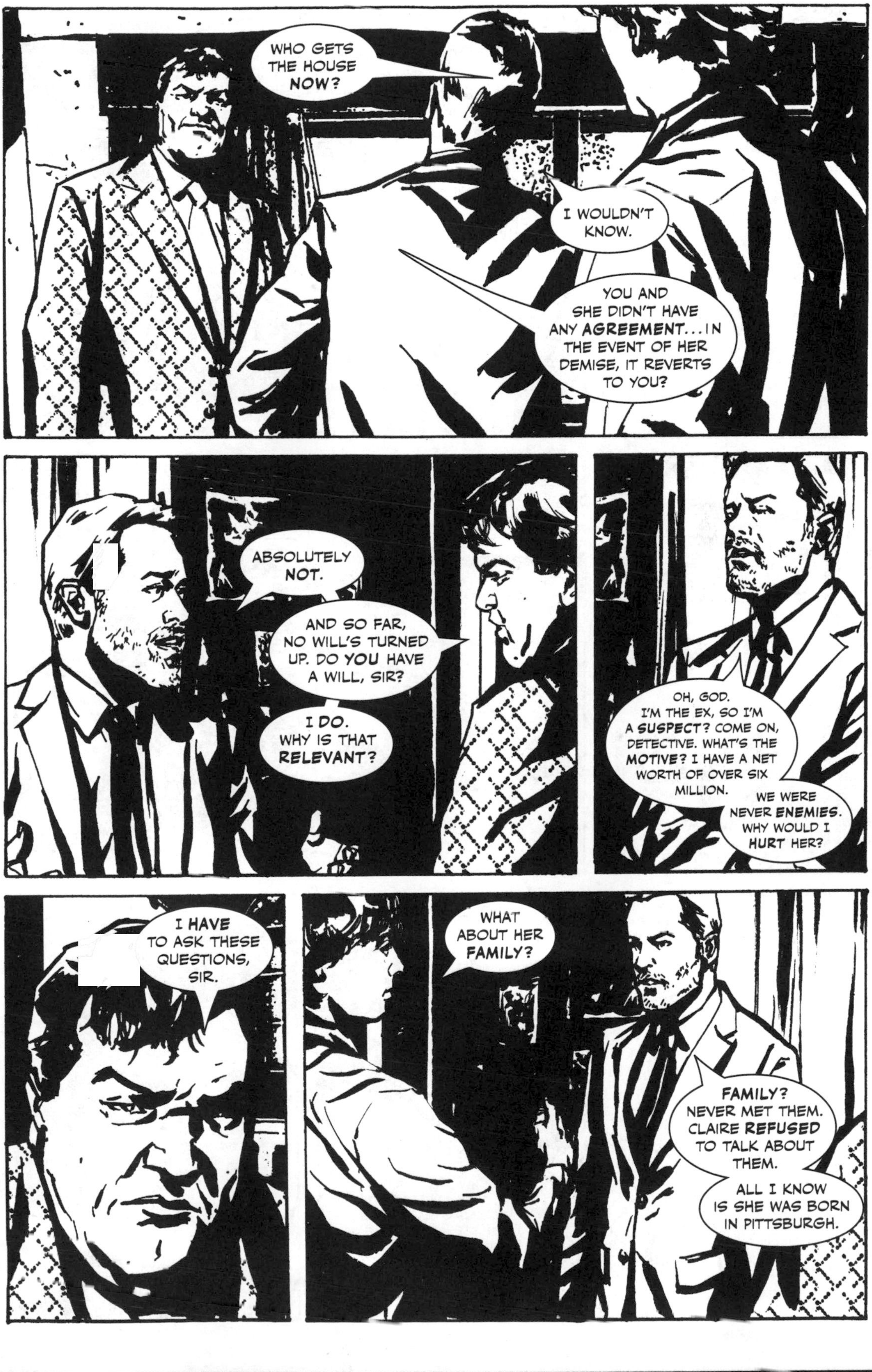
WHO GETS THE HOUSE NOW?
I WOULDN'T KNOW.
YOU AND SHE DIDN'T HAVE ANY AGREEMENT...IN THE EVENT OF HER DEMISE, IT REVERTS TO YOU?
ABSOLUTELY NOT.
AND SO FAR, NO WILL'S TURNED UP. DO YOU HAVE A WILL, SIR?
I DO. WHY IS THAT RELEVANT?
OH, GOD. I'M THE EX, SO I'M A SUSPECT? COME ON, DETECTIVE. WHAT'S THE MOTIVE? I HAVE A NET WORTH OF OVER SIX MILLION.
WE WERE NEVER ENEMIES. WHY WOULD I HURT HER?
I HAVE TO ASK THESE QUESTIONS, SIR.
WHAT ABOUT HER FAMILY?
FAMILY? NEVER MET THEM. CLAIRE REFUSED TO TALK ABOUT THEM.
ALL I KNOW IS SHE WAS BORN IN PITTSBURGH.

TWO YEARS OF MARRIAGE, AND SHE NEVER TALKED ABOUT HER **FAMILY** AT ALL?

THAT'S **RIGHT.** SHE WAS A CLOSED BOOK. EVERY TIME I TRIED TO GET PERSONAL, SHE CHANGED THE SUBJECT.

AND, SHE HAD AN **INTERESTING** WAY OF DOING SO.

WHAT WAS THAT?

SHE TOOK ME TO BED.

MILO CONVINCED HIM TO LOOK AROUND THE REST OF THE HOUSE. STARGILL REACHED HIS LIMIT IN THE BEDROOM, WHEN MILO TOLD HIM CLAIRE'S CLOTHES HAD BEEN TAKEN TO THE CRIME LAB.

HE HANDED US A CARTON OF DOCUMENTS FROM THE BACKSEAT OF THE BMW, AND TOOK OFF.

SO, WHAT'S YOUR TAKE?

HE'S GOT HIS SHARE OF **PROBLEMS,** BUT NO BELLS ARE RINGING, AND WHERE'S THE MOTIVE?

THREE HUNDRED GRAND AFTER TAXES IS **STILL** SERIOUS BREAD, AND GUYS WITH BIG NET WORTHS CAN STILL GET INTO TROUBLE. I'M GOING TO TAKE A CRASH COURSE ON HIS FINANCES.

WHAT DO YOU MEAN, **PROBLEMS?**

IT TAKES A CERTAIN KIND OF **SELF-ABSORPTION** TO STAY IN A RELATIONSHIP LIKE THAT, EVEN FOR A COUPLE OF YEARS.

SOUNDS MORE LIKE A PASSION-WITH-A-STRANGER **FANTASY** GONE WRONG THAN A **MARRIAGE.**

THEY WERE BOTH **IMPULSIVE.**

STARGILL SAYS THEY ENDED UP AVOIDING EACH OTHER.

MAYBE THEY **BOTH** HAD AFFAIRS.

CLAIRE COULD HAVE BEEN DATING **STRANGERS** FOR YEARS. MAYBE SHE MET THE WRONG ONE.

NEIGHBORS NEVER SAW A THING.

MAYBE SHE TOOK THEM SOMEWHERE ELSE.

ONE THING STARGILL TOLD US: CLAIRE LOVED **CONTROL.**

SHE CON-TROLLED HIM THROUGH SEX. WHEN THAT LOST ITS APPEAL, SHE DECIDED TO END IT, AND ON HER TERMS.

MAYBE SHE FOUND A NUTCASE WHO'D GOTTEN OUT OF THE HOSPITAL, TRIED TO CONTROL HIM...**DOMINATE** HIM, EVEN. PRESSED THE WRONG BUTTON.

BRNG-BRNG

OR, IT COULD STILL TURN OUT TO BE A CARJACKING GONE—

MILO STEPPED AWAY TO ANSWER HIS CELL PHONE.

A MINUTE LATER HE TURNED BACK AS HE ENDED THE CALL.

THAT WAS YOUNG MISS OTT. SHE'S ON THE NIGHT SHIFT AT STARKWEATHER...WANTS TO **TALK** BEFORE WORK.

TALK ABOUT **WHAT?**

SHE WOULDN'T **SAY,** BUT I KNOW **SCARED** WHEN I HEAR IT.

SHE'D ASKED TO MEET AT PLUMMER PARK IN WEST HOLLYWOOD.

THANKS FOR COMING. MY ROOM-MATE'S SLEEPING, OR I WOULD'VE HAD YOU COME TO MY PLACE.

IF I HADN'T BEEN LOOKING FOR THE FEAR, I MIGHT NOT HAVE NOTICED IT. SHE WORE IT LIGHTLY...A GLAZE OF ANXIETY.

SHE WAITED NERVOUSLY FOR A GAUNT MAN WITH LONG HAIR TO PASS WITH HIS DOG, EVERY STEP SEEMING TO STRAIN THE ANIMAL.

I'M PROBABLY **WASTING** YOUR TIME. IT'S **JUST**... CAN I ASK YOU SOMETHING?

SURE.

CLAIRE...DR. ARGENT...WAS ANYTHING DONE TO HER EYES?

THERE WAS, WASN'T THERE? OH MY GOD.

WHAT ABOUT HER EYES **CONCERNS** YOU, MS. OTT?

36

OKAY, THIS IS GOING TO SOUND **WEIRD** BUT, THREE DAYS AGO...THE DAY BEFORE CLAIRE WAS KILLED...ONE OF THE **PATIENTS** SAID SOMETHING.

THIS IS A PATIENT CLAIRE WORKED WITH. HE **NEVER** SAYS ANYTHING. HE'S BARELY VERBAL. YOU...YOU'RE GOING TO THINK I'M PARANOID.

NOT AT ALL.

OKAY. I'M ABOUT TO LEAVE HIS ROOM AND THIS GUY STARTS **MUMBLING.** THEN, ALL OF A SUDDEN, HE SAYS HER NAME.

"DR. A," HE SAYS. "DR. A. BAD EYES IN A BOX."

I SEE. WHAT'S THIS PATIENT'S NAME?

YOU'RE GOING TO **PURSUE** IT? LISTEN...I DON'T WANT TO MAKE WAVES. WE'RE NOT SUPPOSED TO GIVE OUT NAMES.

MA'AM, IT'S IMPORTANT. IF THERE'S ANY CHANCE THIS MAN—

THERE'S JUST NO WAY. HE'S BEEN LOCKED UP FOR YEARS. HE SEES NO ONE.

IT'S...IT'S ARDIS PEAKE. MAYBE YOU'VE HEARD OF HIM. CLAIRE SAID HE WAS **NOTORIOUS.** THE PAPERS GAVE HIM A NICKNAME.

MONSTER.

MILO'S JAW WAS TOO SMOOTH. FORCED RELAXATION.

I'VE HEARD OF PEAKE.

SO HAD I.

HEIDI OTT HAD BEEN A GRADE-SCHOOL KID. HER PARENTS WOULD HAVE SHIELDED HER FROM THE DETAILS.

I REMEMBERED THE FACTS THE PAPERS HAD PRINTED, WHETHER I **WANTED** TO OR NOT.

A FARM TOWN AN HOUR NORTH OF L.A.: TREADWAY. A **PRETTY** PLACE WHERE PEOPLE STILL LEFT THEIR DOORS UNLOCKED.

ARDIS PEAKE'S MOTHER WORKED AS A MAID AND COOK FOR A PROMINENT RANCH FAMILY.

ARDIS WAS NINETEEN. ILLITERATE, PRETER-NATURALLY SHY. **DIFFERENT.** HE LIVED ALONE IN A ONE-ROOM SHACK BEHIND A PEACH ORCHARD.

HE GOT IN **TROUBLE:** PAINT-SNIFFING AND SUCH. BROAD-DAYLIGHT ACTS SO RECKLESS THEY CONFIRMED HIS REPUTATION AS **RETARDED.**

SO, THE RANCH OWNERS KEPT HIM BUSY WITH A **JOB** OF SORTS: RAT CATCHER, GOPHER KILLER, SNAKE BUTCHER. THE FARM'S HUMAN TERRIER.

A DOG'S JOB ASSIGNED TO A MAN, BUT BY ALL ACCOUNTS ARDIS PEAKE HAD FOUND HIS NICHE.

IT ALL **ENDED** ON A COOL, SWEET SUNDAY MORNING.

IT WASN'T UNCOMMON FOR ARDIS'S MOTHER NOREEN TO STAY UP ALL NIGHT COOKING.

THE INCISION THAT HAD REMOVED HER HEAD WAS SLOPPY.

THE YOUNG RANCHER AND HIS WIFE WERE STILL IN BED UPSTAIRS, THEIR HEADS STILL ATTACHED.

THE BIG KNIFE HAD SEARED THROUGH FLESH, BUT FAILED AT BONE.

MR. AND MRS. ARDULLO. YOUNG AND GOOD-LOOKING. A GOLDEN COUPLE WITH EVERYTHING TO LIVE FOR.

HE'D BEEN A SLUGGER IN HIGH SCHOOL.

THE COUPLE'S DAUGHTER HAD LIKELY HEARD SOMETHING AND HID IN THE CLOSET. IT HADN'T SAVED HER.

A PLAYROOM SEPARATED THE GIRL'S ROOM FROM THE BABY'S.

THE BABY WAS AN EIGHT-MONTH-OLD BOY. HIS CRIB WAS EMPTY.

THE TRAIL OF RED SNEAKER **PRINTS** LED ALONG THE PATH TO THE ORCHARD, TO ARDIS PEAKE'S SHACK. HE WAS FOUND THERE, NAKED AND UNCONSCIOUS, SURROUNDED BY EMPTY PAINT CANS, GLUE TUBES, AND BOTTLES OF MEXICAN VODKA. A PLASTIC PACKET OF METHAMPHETAMINE WAS FOUND UNDER THE COT.

PEAKE WAS FAST ASLEEP, **DRENCHED** IN BLOOD AND BITS OF CEREBRAL TISSUE. POLICE INITIALLY THOUGHT HE WAS ANOTHER VICTIM. LATER, EVERYTHING **WASHED** OFF.

A **SCORCHING** SMELL COMPOUNDED THE REEK OF OFFAL, PUTRID FOOD AND UNWASHED CLOTHES. A HOT PLATE POWERED BY AN OLD CAR BATTERY. A TIN WASTEBASKET SERVING AS A SAUCEPAN HAD BEEN LEFT ON THE HEAT.

SOMETHING ELSE. HEADY. A **STEW**. THE BABY'S PAJAMAS ON THE FLOOR, COVERED BY FLIES.

ARDIS PEAKE HAD NEVER BEEN ONE FOR **COOKING**. HIS MOTHER HAD ALWAYS TAKEN CARE OF THAT.

THIS MORNING, HE'D **TRIED**.

I'D NEVER HEARD OF HIM **BEFORE** I CAME TO STARKWEATHER. CLAIRE TOLD ME ABOUT... WHAT HE **DID.**

THIS EYE THING...IT'S **NOTHING,** RIGHT?

PROBABLY NOTHING, BUT I WILL WANT TO TALK TO PEAKE.

GOOD **LUCK** WITH THAT. IT TOOK CLAIRE AND ME **MONTHS** JUST TO GET HIS ATTENTION.

BETTER BRACE MYSELF FOR A **LECTURE** FROM SWIG. I PROBABLY SHOULD HAVE GONE THROUGH HIM ON THIS.

NOT THAT IT REALLY **MATTERS.** I'M MOVING ON, ANYWAY. I'VE HAD MY FILL OF STARKWEATHER.

BEFORE YOU GO, MAYBE YOU COULD **HELP** US...TRY TO DRAW PEAKE OUT AGAIN. THINK OF IT AS A **CHALLENGE.**

I'M **OVER** CHALLENGES WHEN IT COMES TO THAT PLACE. IF I WANT A CHALLENGE NOW, I ROCK-CLIMB.

I'M **AFRAID** OF HEIGHTS.

YOU GET USED TO IT. THAT'S THE **POINT.** I LIKE ALL SORTS OF PHYSICAL CHALLENGES...CLIMBING, PARASAILING, SKY-DIVING.

LITTLE MS. DAREDEVIL? "DR. A BAD EYES IN A BOX." WHAT IF IT'S **NOT** PURE GIBBERISH? WHAT IF PEAKE HAD A BUDDY WHO GOT OUT?

IT DOESN'T SOUND LIKE PEAKE **HAS** BUDDIES. BUT **MAYBE**. WE SHOULD HAVE A CLOSER LOOK AT HIM.

YEAH. AND, THERE'S SOMETHING **ELSE**, ALEX.

AT QUANTICO, PEAKE'S CASE SUMMARY WAS PASSED AROUND. I REMEMBER SEASONED GUYS BLANCHING WHEN THEY SAW THE PHOTOS. IT WAS **BEYOND** BUTCHERY.

I WASN'T A HARDENED **BASTARD** YET. ALL I COULD DO WAS SKIM.

WHAT?

ONE OF THE **PHOTOS**. THE OLDER CHILD. PEAKE TOOK THE **EYES**.

WE MADE THE TRIP **BACK** TO STARKWEATHER. SWIG DIDN'T LIKE IT... INSISTED THERE WAS **NO** WAY PEAKE HAD SAID ANYTHING MEANINGFUL.

PEAKE WAS WITHDRAWN, SEVERELY ASOCIAL AND **EXTREMELY** LOW-FUNCTIONING. HE'D ALSO HAD NO MAIL OR OTHER CONTACT WITH THE OUTSIDE WORLD FOR YEARS.

AND...SWIG HAD CHECKED: NO ONE HAD BEEN **RELEASED** FROM STARKWEATHER SINCE CLAIRE ARGENT HAD COME ON BOARD.

MILO PRESSED FOR A MEETING WITH PEAKE ANYWAY, AND SWIG EVENTUALLY RELENTED.

ROOM 15 S & R

HERE WE ARE, THEN.

SUPPRESSION AND RESTRAINT?

NOT BECAUSE HE **NEEDS** IT. THE ROOMS ARE SMALLER, SO WE USE THEM FOR PATIENTS WHO LIVE ALONE.

HE LIVES ALONE BECAUSE HIS **HYGIENE** IS...WELL, YOU'LL GET TO EXPERIENCE THAT FOR YOURSELVES.

THERE WE ARE.

GENTLE-MEN...

...HE'S ALL YOURS.

MUSIC CAME FROM SOMEWHERE IN THE CEILING. SUGARY STRINGS AND BELCHING HORNS. SOME LONG-FORGOTTEN FORTIES POP TUNE IN A MAJOR KEY, PLAYED BY A BAND THAT DIDN'T CARE.

SWIG HADN'T EXAGGERATED ABOUT THE **SMELL**. VINEGARY SWEAT, FLATULENCE AND BURNING RUBBER. SOMETHING DEAD.

AS WE STEPPED IN, PEAKE LIFTED HIS HEAD. A DARK, WET **TONGUE** SHOWED ITSELF, FILLING A TINY, LIPLESS MOUTH. HIS CHEEKS BELLOWED, CAVED IN, INFLATED AGAIN. HIS NECK ROLLED TO THE LEFT AS HIS EYES CLOSED. THE TONGUE WITHDREW AND THE MOUTH OPENED. LOTS OF TEETH MISSING.

A LIVING **SKELETON**. I'D SEEN A FACE LIKE THAT SOMEWHERE.

HE'D BUTCHERED THE ARDULLOS AT AGE NINETEEN, MAKING HIM THIRTY-FIVE NOW. HE LOOKED **ANCIENT**. SWIG SAID THE NAME, "ARDIS?" MORE TONGUE THRUSTS WERE THE ONLY REPLY.

I KNEW **WHERE** I'D SEEN THE FACE. POSTER ART FROM MY COLLEGE DAYS. EDVARD MUNCH'S **THE SCREAM**. PEAKE COULD HAVE POSED FOR THE PAINTING.

MILO SPOKE WITH SURPRISING GENTLENESS.

HEY. ARDIS. MY NAME'S MILO. I'M A **DETECTIVE**. I'M HERE TO ASK YOU ABOUT DR. ARGENT.

I'M A HOMICIDE DE-TECTIVE, ARDIS. HOMICIDE.

THE **MOVEMENTS** CONTINUED... HEAD ROLLING, TONGUE DARTING. ALL OF IT AUTONOMIC, DEVOID OF CONTENT.

THE BURNING SMELL GREW STRONGER.

ARDIS! CLAIRE ARGENT. DR. ARGENT. BAD EYES IN A BOX.

MILO WAITED A FULL MINUTE FOR A RESPONSE. PEAKE'S NEUROPATHIC BALLET CONTINUED, UNALTERED.

I LOOKED INTO PEAKE'S EYES. PLUMBING FOR SOME SHRED OF A SOUL.

FLAT BLACK. LIGHTS OUT. ONCE UPON A TIME HE'D **DESTROYED** AN ENTIRE FAMILY, TAKING THE EYES OF ONE.

NOW HIS WERE TWIN PORTHOLES ON A SHIP TO **NOWHERE**. AS IF SOMEONE HAD SNIPPED THE WIRES CONNECTING BODY TO SOUL.

SATISFIED?

WHY DON'T WE GIVE **HEIDI** A TRY WITH HIM?

SWIG AGREED TO SUMMON HEIDI. HE ATTEMPTED TO ASSERT HIS AUTHORITY BY LIMITING HER TIME WITH PEAKE TO TEN MINUTES.

THIS IS ENTIRELY POINTLESS.

MAYBE, SIR, BUT I'D BE DERELICT IF I DIDN'T FOLLOW UP ON IT.

OTT STAYED IN THE ROOM FOR NEARLY TWENTY. WHEN SHE EMERGED, SHE SHOOK HER HEAD.

ROOM 15 S&R

NOTHING. I'M SORRY. SHOULD I TRY LONGER?

THAT'S MORE THAN ENOUGH, MS. OTT. I THINK, DETECTIVE, IT'S TIME FOR ALL OF US TO GET BACK TO WORK.

WE WERE USHERED OUT, THIS TIME BY SWIG HIMSELF.

AFTER A COUPLE OF DAYS, I'VE HAD MORE THAN ENOUGH OF THIS PLACE. CAN YOU IMAGINE COMING EVERY DAY?

AND PEAKE... WHAT THE HELL TURNS A HUMAN BEING INTO THAT?

ANSWER THAT AND YOU'VE GOT THE NOBEL.

WHY DO SOME SCHIZOPHRENICS BECOME VIOLENT? DOPE AND BOOZE WERE IN PLAY FOR PEAKE, BUT MAYBE A RANDOM CIRCUIT IN HIS BRAIN JUST SHORTED OUT.

WE JUST DON'T KNOW WHY SOME PSYCHOTICS BLOW.

GREAT. I'LL NEVER BE OUT OF WORK.

MILO AND I HAD AGREED TO **DIVVY** UP THE CASE WORK. HE'D LOOK INTO CLAIRE'S FINANCES, AND STARGILL'S. HE'D ALSO DIVE BACK INTO THE DADA FILE, LOOKING FOR SOMETHING HE'D MISSED THE FIRST **HUNDRED** TIMES.

I'D TALK TO **CLAIRE'S** FORMER CO-WORKERS AND SUPERVISOR. BY 9:45 THE NEXT MORNING I WAS CLEARING MY HEAD IN THE FAST LANE OF THE 10 EAST, MOVING WITH THE SMOG STREAM TO SAN BERNADINO. COUNTY GENERAL HOSPITAL SAT IN EAST L.A. A DUN-COLORED METROPOLIS.

I'D DONE SOME CLINICAL TRAINING THERE, BUT IT HAD BEEN TWO YEARS SINCE I'D SET FOOT ON THE CAMPUS. OUTWARDLY, NOTHING HAD CHANGED... THE SAME **SPRAWL** OF BULKY, HOMELY BUILDINGS, THE CONSTANT **PARADE** OF PEOPLE IN UNIFORMS, THE HALTING MARCH OF THE ILL.

I SPOKE WITH CLAIRE ARGENT'S FORMER SUPERVISOR, FOUND NOTHING NEW. CLAIRE WAS A LONER. **DETACHED.** COLD, BUT EFFECTIVE.

SHE SECURED HER GRANTS AND WENT ABOUT HER WORK, RIGHT UP UNTIL THE DAY SHE JUST WALKED AWAY.

REMINISCENT OF HOW SHE'D DIVORCED JOE STARGILL.

I FOUND A FORMER CO-WORKER ON THE WAY OUT: DR. MARY HERTZLINGER. SHE'D WORKED WITH CLAIRE FOR YEARS, AND FELT SHE HADN'T REALLY KNOWN HER.

THERE WAS **SOME-THING**...SOMETHING SHE SAID ON HER WAY OUT THE DOOR, LITERALLY. SOME-THING ABOUT GOING TO STARKWEATHER.

IT STUCK WITH ME, BECAUSE SHE SAID IT WITH A **SMILE.**

"SO MANY **MAD-MEN**," SHE SAID, "AND SO LITTLE **TIME.**"

MILO HAD GONE BACK TO CLAIRE'S HOUSE FOR THE REMAINING SCRAPS OF FINANCIAL DATA. I MET HIM THERE AFTER LEAVING COUNTY.

MADMEN? WHY? TO SQUEEZE A FEW MORE **SYLLABLES** OUT OF THEM?

I'M CONCENTRATING ON THE **BORING** STUFF. LOCATED A SAFE-DEPOSIT BOX AT HER BANK. STONE EMPTY.

AND, STILL **NOTHING** OF NOTE IN THE PAPERS I'VE BEEN PULLING FROM HER OFFICE. IF SHE HAD SOME KIND OF **SECRET** LIFE GOING, SHE KEPT IT VERY WELL WRAPPED.

HER **PARENTS** ARE COMING IN TO-MORROW. YOU SHOULD BE WITH ME WHEN I MEET THEM.

I'VE BEEN REVIEWING RICHARD DADA'S FILE, AS WELL. **SOBERING.** I TOOK ANOTHER CRACK AT THE FILM OUTFIT HE MIGHT'VE AUDITIONED FOR...THIN LINE. ZIP.

EVEN FLY-BY-NIGHTS NEED **EQUIPMENT.** A SMALL OUTFIT MIGHT BE MORE LIKELY TO **RENT.** WHAT ABOUT LEASING COMPANIES?

THAT'S **GOOD.** THANK YOU, SIR. I'LL START **DIGGING.** WHAT'RE YOU UP TO?

CAN'T GET PEAKE OUT OF MY MIND...

"...THOUGHT I'D DO SOME RESEARCH."

I DROVE TO WESTWOOD AND USED THE COMPUTERS AT THE U'S RESEARCH LIBRARY TO LOOK UP THE ARDULLO MASSACRE. THE **PERIODICALS** INDEX OFFERED HALF A PAGE OF CITATIONS, AND I WENT LOOKING FOR MICROFICHE. MOST OF THE ARTICLES WERE NEARLY IDENTICALLY WORDED, LIFTED INTACT FROM WIRE SERVICE REPORTS.

AN ARREST HEADSHOT SHOWED A YOUNG ARDIS PEAKE... THE **MONSTER** HIMSELF. A CORNERED ANIMAL. THE EDVARD MUNCH SCREAMER ON JET FUEL. A LARGE BRUISE SPREAD BENEATH HIS LEFT EYE. THE LEFT SIDE OF HIS FACE SWELLED. ROUGH ARREST?

THE FACTS WERE AS I **REMEMBERED** THEM. MULTIPLE STAB WOUNDS, CRUSHING SKULL FRACTURES, EXTENSIVE MUTILATION, CANNIBALISM. THE ARTICLES FILLED IN NAMES AND PLACES. **DETAILS** ON THE FAMILY.

SCOTT AND THERESA ARDULLO, THIRTY-THREE AND TWENTY-NINE, RESPECTIVELY. MARRIED SIX YEARS, BOTH UC DAVIS AGRICULTURAL GRADS. BRITTANY, FIVE YEARS OLD. JUSTIN, EIGHT MONTHS.

NEXT CAME THE HAPPIER-TIMES FAMILY **PORTRAIT**. SCOTT ARDULLO HAD BEEN MUSCULAR, BLOND. THE SMILE OF ONE WHO TRULY BELIEVES HIMSELF **BLESSED**.

HIS WIFE, SLENDER, SOMEWHAT PLAIN. HER EXPRESSION SEEMED SOMEHOW LESS **CERTAIN** OF HAPPY ENDINGS. I COULDN'T BEAR TO LOOK AT THE CHILDREN'S FACES.

QUOTES FROM TREADWAY'S SHERIFF, JACOB HAAS. "I SERVED IN KOREA AND THIS WAS WORSE THAN ANYTHING I SAW OVER THERE. IT'S JUST BEYOND BELIEF."

ANONYMOUS TOWNSPEOPLE CITED PEAKE'S STRANGE HABITS. HE MUMBLED TO HIMSELF, DIDN'T BATHE, CRUISED ALLEYS, ATE DUMPSTER TRASH. EVERYONE HAD KNOWN OF HIS FONDNESS FOR SNIFFING GLUE. NO ONE HAD THOUGHT HIM DANGEROUS.

ONE OTHER ATTRIBUTED QUOTE, FROM LOCAL YOUTH, DERRICK CRIMMINS. "HE DIDN'T HANG OUT WITH ANYONE. NO ONE WANTED TO HANG WITH HIM BECAUSE HE SMELLED BAD AND HE WAS JUST TOO WEIRD, MAYBE INTO SATAN OR SOMETHING."

NO OTHER MENTION OF SATANIC RITUALS, AND I WONDERED IF THERE'D BEEN ANY FOLLOW-UP. PROBABLY NOT, WITH PEAKE OUT OF CIRCULATION. I KEPT SPOOLING, FOUND BRIEF MENTION OF PEAKE'S COMMITMENT TO STARKWEATHER.

USING "TREADWAY" AS A KEYWORD PULLED UP NOTHING SINCE THE MURDERS. QUIET TOWN. EXTINCT TOWN. HOW DID AN ENTIRE COMMUNITY DIE? HAD PEAKE SOMEHOW KILLED IT, TOO?

THE FLIGHT INN SAT NEAR LAX, TOO **LARGE** TO BE A MOTEL, IT SOMEHOW HADN'T PASSED THOUGH HOTEL PUBERTY.

A 747 ROARED OVERHEAD.

MILO ANSWERED MY KNOCK AT THE DOOR TO ROOM 129. HE LOOKED WEARY.

NO PROGRESS, OR SOMETHING **ELSE**?

MILO MADE THE **INTRODUCTIONS**. ERNESTINE AND ROBERT RAY ARGENT. BOTH OF THEM HAD THAT SOFT, DISTINCTIVE PITTSBURGH DRAWL.

THE ROOM WAS ICY, BUT ROBERT RAY'S FOREHEAD WAS BEADED, DRIPPING.

SO, YOU'RE A **PSYCHOLOGIST**, LIKE CLAIRE.

YES.

HE NODDED, AS IF WE'D REACHED SOME AGREEMENT.

MILO SAID HE'D BEEN FILLING THE ARGENTS IN ON THE COURSE OF THE INVESTIGATION.

AT THE MENTION OF THE WORD, ERNESTINE GAVE A SMALL, INVOLUNTARY CRY. ROBERT RAY OFFERED SUCCINCT SUPPORT. "HONEY."

CLAIRE **LOVED** PSYCHOLOGY.

SHE WAS ALL WE EVER **REALLY** HAD.

SO, WHAT'S THE CHANCE YOU FIND THE **DEVIL** WHO DID THIS?

I'M **ALWAYS** OPTIMISTIC, SIR. THE MORE YOU AND MRS. ARGENT CAN TELL US ABOUT CLAIRE, THE BETTER OUR CHANCES.

WHEN WAS THE LAST TIME YOU SAW CLAIRE?

CHRISTMAS. SHE **ALWAYS** CAME HOME FOR CHRISTMAS. WE ALWAYS HAD A NICE **FAMILY** TIME, NO EXCEPTION LAST CHRISTMAS. SHE HELPED HER MOTHER WITH THE COOKING.

SO, HALF A YEAR AGO.

THAT WOULD BE RIGHT AROUND THE TIME CLAIRE LEFT COUNTY HOS-PITAL AND MOVED TO STARKWEATHER HOSPITAL.

BLANK STARES. THE ARGENTS HADN'T KNOWN. MILO MOVED ON.

HOW LONG DID SHE **STAY** AT HOME DURING THE HOLIDAY?

WHAT ROB RAY'S SAYING IS, SHE WAS **KIND** AND GENEROUS. NO ONE COULD HAVE **HATED** HER.

FOUR DAYS, LIKE ALWAYS. WE WENT TO A BUNCH OF MOVIES. SHE **LOVED** HER MOVIES.

I DON'T SEE WHAT THIS...THERE'S NO REASON FOR ANY-ONE TO WANT TO **HURT** HER.

GENEROUS TO THE NTH-DEGREE. ALWAYS THE FIRST TO VOLUNTEER TO HELP OTHERS. SHE LOVED **ANIMALS** ESPECIALLY.

IT DOESN'T MAKE **SENSE**, DETECTIVE STURGIS. AT THE MORGUE...WHAT WE SAW.

I JUST DON'T...IT HAD TO BE A **MANIAC**. THIS STARKWEATHER PLACE IS NOTHING BUT MANIACS?

YES, SIR. IT'S THE FIRST THING WE LOOKED AT. SO FAR, NO LEADS.

WHAT ABOUT HER **MARRIAGE**? AND THE **DIVORCE**. ANYTHING I SHOULD KNOW ABOUT THAT?

WE...WE DON'T KNOW **MUCH**. SHE SAID SHE'D GOTTEN MARRIED IN RENO. WE NEVER MET HIM.

I'M **SURE** WE WOULD'VE, BUT CLAIRE DIDN'T STAY MARRIED TO HIM VERY LONG.

TWO YEARS, NO CONTACT.

I KNOW THIS SOUNDS **WEIRD**...OUR NOT MEETING HIM. BUT CLAIRE **ALWAYS** NEEDED HER FREEDOM.

PRIVACY'S A BIG THING WITH HER, SO WE TRY TO **RESPECT** THAT.

THE LAPSE INTO **PRESENT** TENSE MADE MY OWN EYES BEGIN TO ACHE.

HE MIGHT'VE REALIZED IT, TOO. HIS SHOULDERS LOWERED SUDDENLY, AS IF SOMEONE HAD PUSHED THEM DOWN.

I DON'T WANT YOU TO THINK CLAIRE WAS SOME STRANGE KID. SHE WAS JUST...**TOUGH**. TOOK CARE OF HERSELF. THIS HAD TO BE AN ABDUCTION, SOME KIND OF MANIAC.

CLAIRE WAS NO **FOOL**. SHE KNEW HOW TO TAKE CARE OF HERSELF...**HAD** TO KNOW.

BECAUSE SHE LIVED ALONE?

BECAUSE... YES, **EXACTLY**. MY LITTLE GIRL WAS **INDEPENDENT**.

SO MUCH PAIN.

OH, **MAN**. THEY SEEM LIKE GOOD PEOPLE, BUT TALK ABOUT **DELUSIONS**.

JUST ONE BIG, **HAPPY** FAMILY. NEVER MIND THAT CLAIRE **NEVER** BRINGS THE HUSBAND AROUND, **NEVER** CALLS. SHE CUT THEM OFF, ALEX. WHY?

THERE'S **MORE** THERE... SOME FORM OF FAMILY CHAOS. YOU COULD ALMOST **FEEL** THEM DANCING AROUND IT.

YEAH. YOU SAW HOW **DEFENSIVE** THEY GOT ABOUT THE NOTION OF CLAIRE BEING DETACHED.

THEY MAY BE HOLDING BACK FAMILY **SECRETS**, BUT I DON'T THINK THEY'D **OBSTRUCT** YOU.

HER L.A. LIFE STILL SEEMS MORE RELEVANT THAN PITTSBURGH.

BUT, WHAT IF THERE **WAS** SOME FAMILY TRAUMA? WHAT IF SHE'D NEEDED TO **ESCAPE** SOMEHOW?

HER LOVE OF MOVIES?

RIGHT. WHAT IF IT LED TO **MORE** THAN JUST WATCHING?

CAUSED HER TO HAVE **ACTING** ASPIRATIONS? WHAT IF SHE ANSWERED A CASTING CALL... THE **SAME** ONE RICHARD DADA ANSWERED?

I GUESS. SO THEY BOTH MEET SOME LOON ON THE SET... THEN WHY THE TIME LAPSE BETWEEN THE MURDERS?

MAYBE **OTHER** MURDERS WE DON'T KNOW ABOUT?

I LOOKED FOR **SIMILARS**. ANYTHING IN CAR TRUNK, ANYTHING WITH EYE WOUNDS OR SAW MARKS. ZIP.

BUT, **HELL**... NOT LIKE WE HAVE ANYTHING **BETTER** TO GO ON. WANNA MAKE SOME ROUNDS?

THE HOLLYWOOD EQUIPMENT RENTAL OUTFITS WERE IN WAREHOUSE BUILDINGS, BETWEEN FAIRFAX AND GOWER.

A CONCENTRATION ON SANTA MONICA BOULEVARD ALLOWED US TO COVER HALF A DOZEN BUSINESSES ON FOOT. MILO GOT A CALL ON HIS CELL AS WE WERE ENTERING THE SEVENTH.

STATE PAROLE SUPERVISOR RETURNING MY CALL. IT'LL TAKE **DAYS** TO SEARCH ALL THE RECORDS ASSOCIATED WITH STARKWEATHER.

ONE THING SHE DID CONFIRM: STARK-WEATHER GUYS **DO** GET OUT. NOT **OFTEN**, BUT IT HAPPENS.

SHE KNOWS FOR A **FACT** BECAUSE THERE WAS A CASE FIVE YEARS AGO...SOME GUY SUPPOSED TO BE ON CLOSE SUPERVISION SHOT HIMSELF IN A BARBERSHOP.

SO MUCH FOR THE **SYSTEM**. MAYBE THAT'S WHY SWIG IS SO **NERVOUS**.

THE SYSTEM IS **BULLSHIT**. PEOPLE AREN'T MACHINES. EVEN AT QUENTIN OR PELICAN BAY, THERE'S ALL KINDS OF TROUBLE.

EITHER YOU CAGE THEM **COMPLETELY** OR THEY DO WHATEVER THE HELL THEY PLEASE.

WERE YOU **WORKING HERE** TWENTY MONTHS AGO, MISTER...?

BONNER. VITO BONNER.

YEAH. OFF AND ON.

SOUNDS FAMILIAR. YEAH, **MAYBE.** YEAH.

I **GUESS** I CAN LOOK.

REMEMBER RENTING TO AN OUT-FIT CALLED **THIN LINE** PRODUCTIONS?

MAYBE.

· RENTAL COUNTER ·

THE KID RETURNED FROM THE BACK A FEW MINUTES LATER.

YEAH, I **REMEMBER** THEM NOW.

ASSHOLES **STIFFED** US FOR FOURTEEN GRAND.

THAT'S A LOT OF **EQUIP-MENT.**

NOT FOR SPIELBERG, BUT YEAH. WE GAVE 'EM **EVERYTHING.** MIKES, PROPS, FAKE BLOOD, THE FUCKIN' WORKS.

THE BIG ITEMS WERE A DOLLY AND A COUPLE OF CAMERAS... OLD GEAR, NO STUDIO WOULD TOUCH 'EM, BUT **STILL,** THEY COST.

SUPPOSED TO BE A TEN-DAY RENTAL. IT WAS **OBVIOUSLY** LIKE A VIRGIN VOYAGE, SO WE DEMANDED DOUBLE DEPOSIT. GOT A VERIFIED CHECK UPFRONT.

I GOT I.D., EVERYTHING BY THE **BOOK.** NOT ONLY DIDN'T THEY PAY UP, THEY FUCKING **SPLIT** WITH THE EQUIPMENT.

I GUIDED THEM, MAN, TOLD THEM HOW TO GET THE MOST FOR THEIR MONEY. THEN THEY GO AND SCREW ME.

YOU SAY "THEY." HOW MANY PEOPLE ARE WE TALKING ABOUT?

YOU GOT BLAMED?

BOSS SAID I DID THE TRANSACTION, I WAS ASSIGNED TO FIND 'EM, TRY TO RECOVER. I COULDN'T FIND SHIT.

TWO. GUY AND A GIRL.

WHAT'D THEY LOOK LIKE?

TWENTIES, THIRTIES. SHE WAS OKAY-LOOKING. BLOND HAIR. NICE BODY, BUT NOTHING SPECIAL. OKAY FACE.

HE WAS TALL, OLDER THAN HER, TRY-ING TO PLAY HIP. LONG BLACK HAIR. CURLY, LIKE A PERM.

SHIT, THEY WERE BOTH WEAR-ING WIGS, THOUGH.

WASN'T HARD TO TELL.

WHAT KIND OF CLOTHING DID THEY WEAR?

REGULAR. NOTHING SPECIAL.

ANY OTHER DISTINGUISHING MARKS?

LIKE '666' ON THEIR FORE-HEADS? NOPE, UNH-UH.

THE FACT THEY WERE WEARING WIGS. THAT DIDN'T BOTHER YOU?

WHY SHOULD IT? EVERYONE IN THE 'BIZ IS HIDING SOMETHING. YOU NEVER SEE A CHICK WITH A NATURAL RACK ANYMORE, AND HALF THE GUYS ARE WEARING WIGS AND EYE SHADOW.

BIG FUCKING DEAL. MAYBE THEY WERE ACTING IN THEIR OWN FLICK. THAT'S THE WAY IT IS WITH A LOT OF THESE INDIE THINGS.

THEY TELL YOU **ANYTHING** ABOUT THE FLICK? **BLOOD WALK** SOUNDS LIKE A **SLASHER** FLICK.

COULD BE. LIKE I SAID, THEY GOT SOME FAKE BLOOD. I PICKED OUT THE BEST WE HAD. NICE AND THICK.

ANY HINT IT MIGHT'VE BEEN **PORN?**

ANYTHING'S POSSIBLE. I KNOW MOST OF THE PORN PEOPLE, BUT THERE'S ALWAYS NEW ASSHOLES TRYING TO BREAK IN. THEY DIDN'T HAVE THAT VIRGIN PORN FEEL, THOUGH.

THOSE PEOPLE ARE USUALLY STONED- HAPPY ON ECSTASY, BIG FUCKING **ADVENTURE.** RUNNING AT THE MOUTH.

THESE TWO DIDN'T SAY **MUCH.**

THINKING ABOUT IT, THEY DIDN'T **SAY** HARDLY ANYTHING AT ALL.

DO YOU STILL HAVE THEIR FILE?

I DIDN'T THROW IT OUT.

COULD WE PLEASE SEE IT? **PLEASE?**

SURE. THEY RIP SOMEONE **ELSE** OFF? **THAT** WHY YOU'RE HERE?

MAN... TALK ABOUT **STUPID.** WE WARNED ALL THE OTHER COMPANIES. ANYONE WHO RENTED TO THEM AFTER THAT **DESERVES** TO GET CORNHOLED.

1750 Stanford
Santa Monica, CA 9049

Bill To:

Griffith D. Wark
Producer & Preside
THIN LINE PRODS

BOGUS PHONE. **SCAM** FROM THE GET-GO. WARK SOUNDS LIKE A PHONY MONIKER, TOO.

GRIFFITH D. W. TEN TO ONE IT'S AN **INVERSION** OF D. W. GRIFFITH. I'LL ALSO BET THE W IN 'D. W.' WAS WARK. NOT VERY SUBTLE.

CUTE. GETTING LATE. TOMORROW, IT'S ON THE HORN TO THE REST OF THE PROP HOUSES. SEE IF MR. WARK TALKED ANYONE **ELSE** OUT OF GEAR.

YOU LIKE THE **FILM** THING NOW?

WORK WITH WHAT YOU'VE GOT.

I'M AN OLD **STINKHOUND:** WHEN SOMETHING **SMELLS** BAD, I GO NOSING.

COULD HAVE BEEN A **CASTING** SCAM ... GET WANNABES TO PAY FOR AUDITIONS.

WOULDN'T SURPRISE ME. HOLLYWOOD'S ONE BIG SCAM, ANYWAY. IMAGE *ÜBER ALLES,* EVEN WHEN IT'S SUPPOSEDLY LEGIT.

YEAH, THIS WARK FOUND THE RIGHT BUSINESS FOR A PSYCHOPATH. THE ONLY QUESTION IS HOW RELEVANT HIS MIS-CHIEF IS TO MY CASES."

I WOKE UP THE NEXT MORNING THINKING ABOUT CLAIRE'S DECISION TO MOVE TO STARKWEATHER. WHY *NOW*? WHY *THERE*?

SOMETHING DIDN'T *FIT*. I PACED MY OFFICE, TRYING TO COLLATE. ROBIN AND SPIKE WERE OUT, AND THE SILENCE CHEWED AT ME.

BRINNG-BRINNG

THE PHONE RING WAS *GLASS* SHATTERING ON *STONE*.

MILO OFFERED UPDATES. STARGILL HAD AT LEAST FOUR MILLION IN THE BANK, REDUCING HIS MOTIVES TO NIL. NO PROGRESS ON WARK.

THE BLOOD WALK SCRIPT HAD NOT BEEN REGISTERED WITH ANY OF THE GUILDS, AND NO ONE HAD HEARD OF THIN LINE.

BUSY DAY.

YEAH, WITH *ZIPPO* TO SHOW FOR IT.

I'M LOSING INTEREST IN THE MOVIE ANGLE, ESPECIALLY GIVEN WHAT *ELSE* I LEARNED. SOMEONE *WAS* RELEASED FROM STARKWEATHER.

GUY NAMED WENDELL PELLEY, CUT LOOSE THREE WEEKS *BEFORE* CLAIRE GOT THERE.

THAT WOULD BE A MONTH *AFTER* RICHARD DADA'S MURDER.

I GUESS WE COULD BE LOOKING AT *TWO* KILLERS. WHAT'S PELLEY'S BACKGROUND?

WHITE MALE, FORTY-SIX, COMMITTED FOR SHOOTING HIS GIRLFRIEND AND HER THREE LITTLE KIDS UP IN THE SIERRAS.

HE WAS DOING SOME MINING. GOT DRUNK AND WENT *BERSERK*. PARANOID SCHIZOPHRENIC, DRUG AND BOOZE HISTORY, TOO WACKY FOR TRIAL.

SWIG HAD TO SIGN OFF ON THE RELEASE, SO HE HELD BACK PLENTY. SCHMUCK.

MAYBE CLAIRE VISITED STARKWEATHER BEFORE SHE TOOK THE JOB, MET PELLEY, AND HE BECAME HER OUTPATIENT PROJECT.

WE *KNOW* SHE WAS RIPE FOR IT. "SO MANY MADMEN, SO LITTLE TIME."

AND MAYBE PELLEY AND PEAKE STAYED IN TOUCH SOMEHOW. MAYBE PEAKE TALKED TO HIM BECAUSE THEY HAD SOME KIND OF RAPPORT.

THEY HAD ONE KEY THING IN COMMON: THEY *BOTH* MURDERED *FAMILIES.*

AS GOOD A BASIS FOR FRIEND-SHIP AS I'VE EVER HEARD.

IT'S WORTH *PURSUING,* FOR DAMN SURE. FINDING PELLEY IS AT THE TOP OF MY PRIORITY LIST NOW.

RELEASED IN-MATES ARE SUPPOSED TO GET COUNSELING AND RANDOM DRUG TESTS.

YEAH...*SUP-POSED* TO. PELLEY WAS PLACED AT A HALFWAY HOUSE. THEY HAVEN'T SEEN HIM IN A MONTH. I CALLED HIS PAROLE OFFICER. NO CALLBACK YET.

THIS IS MORE TO MY LIKING THAN MOVIES AND PEAKE'S GIB-BERISH. *BAD* GUY GETS OUT ON THE STREET, *BAD* THINGS HAPPEN.

I HEATED UP SOME OF THE LEFTOVER SOUP AND CHEWED ON A HARD ROLL AS I THOUGHT ABOUT MILO'S ENTHUSIASM FOR WENDELL PELLEY.

HE WAS **CLEAR** FOR THE DADA MURDER, AND HAD USED A **GUN**, NOT A KNIFE. MILO WAS DESPERATE FOR AN ANGLE HE COULD GET HIS HANDS ON.

BRNNG BRNG

IT WAS MARY HERTZLINGER, CLAIRE'S FORMER CO-WORKER.

"DR. DELAWARE? I'M SORRY FOR THE INTRUSION."

"AFTER WE SPOKE, I COULDN'T GET **CLAIRE** OUT OF MY MIND. I KEPT THINKING ABOUT HER REMARK...'SO MANY MADMEN.'"

"THE MORE I THOUGHT ABOUT IT, THE MORE IT BOTHERED ME, BECAUSE CLAIRE HAD NEVER JOKED BEFORE. I TRY NOT TO ANALYZE PEOPLE, BUT ANOMALIES ATTRACT ME. OCCUPATIONAL HAZARD, I SUPPOSE."

"ANOMALIES ALSO MAKE ME WONDER ABOUT ANXIETY. IT'S JUST SPECULATION, BUT SHE JUST RATTLED OFF THAT LINE AS IF SHE'D REHEARSED IT...HAD BEEN RECITING IT TO HERSELF. I MEAN, MOVING TO STARKWEATHER WAS A STRANGE THING TO DO."

"ANYWAY, I TRIED TO THINK BACK ABOUT OTHER ODD BEHAVIOR. I LOOKED IN HER OFFICE AGAIN, AND FOUND SOME BOXES SHE'D LEFT BEHIND. I OPENED ONE. I HOPE THAT WAS OKAY. IT'S JUST THAT...THERE WAS A BAG FULL OF NEWSPAPER CLIPPINGS."

"THEY WERE ALL ABOUT A MASS MURDER THAT TOOK PLACE SIXTEEN YEARS AGO. THE **ARDULLO** FAMILY, KILLED BY A MAN NAMED ARDIS **PEAKE**."

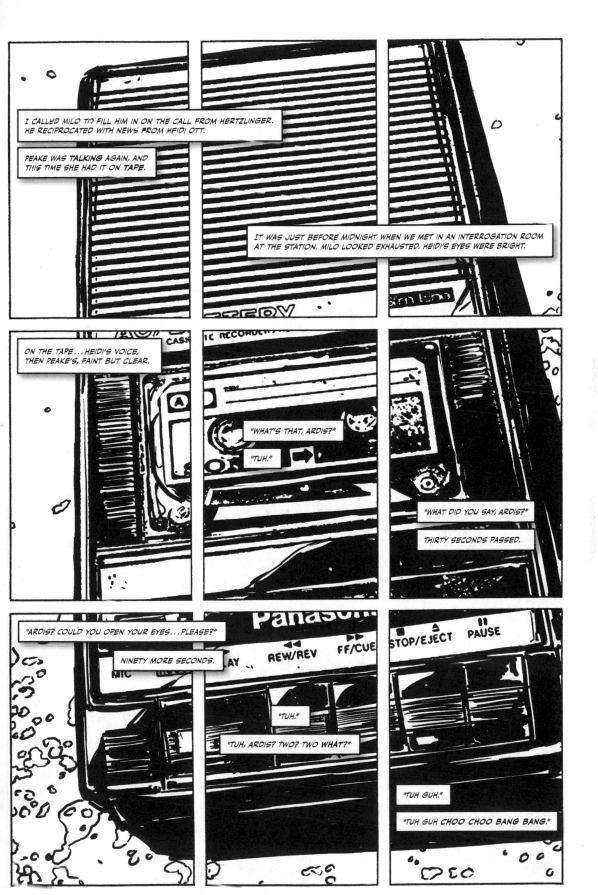

I CALLED MILO TO FILL HIM IN ON THE CALL FROM HERTZLINGER. HE RECIPROCATED WITH NEWS FROM HEIDI OTT.

PEAKE WAS TALKING AGAIN, AND THIS TIME SHE HAD IT ON TAPE.

IT WAS JUST BEFORE MIDNIGHT WHEN WE MET IN AN INTERROGATION ROOM AT THE STATION. MILO LOOKED EXHAUSTED. HEIDI'S EYES WERE BRIGHT.

ON THE TAPE...HEIDI'S VOICE, THEN PEAKE'S, FAINT BUT CLEAR.

"WHAT'S THAT, ARDIS?"

"TUH."

"WHAT DID YOU SAY, ARDIS?"

THIRTY SECONDS PASSED.

"ARDIS? COULD YOU OPEN YOUR EYES...PLEASE?"

NINETY MORE SECONDS.

"TUH."

"TUH, ARDIS? TWO? TWO WHAT?"

"TUH GUH."

"TUH GUH CHOO CHOO BANG BANG."

"CHOO CHOO BANG BANG?"

PRETTY STUPID, ISN'T IT? MAYBE I SHOULDN'T HAVE GOTTEN SO JAZZED. BUT AT LEAST HE'S TALKING TO ME.

DO YOU WANT ME TO KEEP RECORDING HIM?

IT'S GENERALLY ILLEGAL TO TAPE ANY-ONE WITHOUT THEIR KNOWLEDGE.

OKAY. SO I WON'T DO IT ANY-MORE. I'LL JUST... LISTEN.

BEFORE YOU GO, HEIDI... EVER HEAR OF A WENDELL PELLEY?

AN INMATE, RELEASED BE-FORE YOU CAME ON STAFF.

I'VE NEVER HEARD OF HIM, OR OF ANYONE GETTING OUT.

IS HE A SUSPECT IN CLAIRE'S MURDER?

NOT YET. I'M JUST TRYING TO COVER ALL BASES. ANYTHING YOU COULD FIND OUT ABOUT PELLEY WOULD BE USEFUL.

LIKE, DID HE AND PEAKE ASSOCIATE WITH EACH OTHER?

I CAN TRY. ARE YOU SAYING THIS PELLEY IS WHAT PEAKE'S SPEECHES ARE ABOUT? PELLEY SENDING HIM MESSAGES, AND PEAKE BABBLING THEM BACK AT ME?

I WISH I KNEW, HEIDI. RIGHT NOW I'M JUST LOOKING INTO EVERYTHING.

I SLIPPED INTO BED AFTER ONE A.M. VISIONS OF PEAKE'S CRIMES AND THE KNOWLEDGE THAT I HADN'T HELPED MILO MUCH KEPT ME UP FOR A WHILE.

MORNI
NEW

WHEN I WOKE MY LEGS ACHED LIKE I'D BEEN RUNNING FROM SOMETHING. BY NINE I WAS DRINKING COFFEE AND WATCHING WHAT PASSES FOR TV NEWS IN L.A.

I WAS ABOUT TO SWITCH OFF THE SET WHEN THE GRINNING BLONDE GRABBED MY ATTENTION.

AND NOW MORE ON THAT **TRAIN** ACCIDENT.

AN UNIDENTIFIED MAN HAD LAIN ACROSS THE METRORAIL TRACKS EAST OF THE CITY. THE ENGINEER OF A PASSENGER TRAIN TRIED TO PUT ON THE EMERGENCY BRAKE, BUT IT WAS TOO LATE.

CHOO CHOO.

"YEAH, THE LITTLE TRAIN THAT **COULDN'T.** PROBABLY NOTHING. OR MAYBE PEAKE IS A **PROPHET** AND WE SHOULD BE WORSHIPING."

"I CALLED THE CORONER. THE DECEASED IS ELLROY LINCOLN BEATTY, MALE, BLACK, FIFTY-TWO. PETTY CRIMINAL RECORD...POSSESSION AND SUCH."

HE SPENT SOME TIME IN A MENTAL HOSPITAL. CAMARILLO, THIRTEEN YEARS AGO.

WANNA JOIN ME AT THE **MORGUE?** WE CAN HAVE LUNCH LATER. MAYBE A BIG RARE **STEAK.**

"BASICALLY, THE HEAD AND LOWER EXTREMITIES. THE REST IS PRETTY MUCH GOULASH."

...NTY MORGUE
...CIAL BUSINESS ONLY

"IT'S AMAZING WE GOT WHAT WE DID. THE TRAIN MUST HAVE HIT HIM AT WHAT...FORTY, FIFTY MILES PER?"

HOW'D YOU IDENTIFY HIM?

WELFARE CARD IN HIS POCKET. THE LEGS STILL HAD PIECES OF PANTS ON.

YOU COULD STILL SMELL THE BOOZE, EVEN WITH ALL THE OTHER FLUIDS.

I'D LIKE TO LOOK AT BEATTY.

I WANT TO THINK OF HIM AS A PERSON.

A PERSON, HUH? WELL, MAYBE LOOKING AT HIM ISN'T THE RIGHT WAY TO DO THAT, YOU KNOW?

BUT HEY...YOUR CALL.

03

04

ELLROY BEATTY, I PRESUME.

THAT VACANT LOOK COMMON TO ALL DEAD FACES. NO MATTER WHAT YOUR IQ IN LIFE, WHEN THE SOUL FLIES, YOU LOOK STUPID.

WHAT THE **HELL'S** GOING ON HERE? WHO CUT UP MY D.B.?

YOUR D.B.?

THAT'S WHAT I **SAID.** ARE YOU **DEAF,** ALBERT?

I HAD THIS BODY SCHEDULED FOR A POST AND SOMEONE CUT HIS GODDAMN **HEAD** OFF!

NO ONE CUT HIM, THIS IS THE—

BULLSHIT, ALBERT! BULLSHIT ON TOAST! **BULLETS** DON'T SEVER YOUR DAMN HEAD!

THIS IS D.B. **BEATTY.** THE ONE WHO WAS HIT BY A **TRAIN.**

TRAIN?! THIS IS BEATTY, LEROY, AND HE WAS SHOT IN THE HEAD. SAYS SO RIGHT HERE. CASE NUMBER 971132.

NO SIR. WE HAVE THAT CASE NUMBER, BUT IT'S OVER **HERE.**

A **NEW** BODY APPEARED, SAME AS THE FIRST BODY.

EXACT SAME GRAY AS ELLROY BEATTY. SAME **FACE.**

MINOR DISCREPANCIES MATERIALIZED: LEROY BEATTY HAD SLIGHTLY LESS HAIR THAN ELLROY, AND A FULL WHITE BEARD.

THE NEAT, BLACKENED HOLE IN HIS FOREHEAD LOOKED TOO INNOCUOUS TO HAVE KILLED HIM. THE IMPACT HAD LEFT HIM WITH BLOOD-RED EYEBALLS, AS IF HE'D STARED TOO LONG INTO THE FIRES OF HELL.

IT TOOK TWO HOURS TO PUT IT ALL TOGETHER. THERE WAS A LOT OF DR. FRIEDMAN MUTTERING ABOUT HAVING TO WORK WITH INCOMPETENTS.

THE DETECTIVES HANDLING THE TWO DEATH INVESTIGATIONS SHOWED UP. TURNED OUT THE CORPSES WERE... HAD BEEN...BROTHERS.

WHAT'S MORE, ELLROY LINCOLN BEATTY AND LEROY WASHINGTON BEATTY HAD BEEN DISPATCHED AT THE SAME TIME, GIVE OR TAKE TWENTY MINUTES: THREE A.M.

THE COP WHO'D BEEN ASSIGNED TO LEROY ASKED MILO ABOUT OUR CONNECTION TO THE BROTHERS. MILO TOLD HIM HE WOULDN'T **BELIEVE** IT IF HE TRIED.

SO, HOW 'BOUT THAT LUNCH?

NOT IN THE MOOD.

SUCH STRENGTH OF CHARACTER.

"CHOO CHOO BANG BANG." "BAD EYES IN A BOX." TWICE PEAKE SPOUTS OFF THE DAY BEFORE.

SO WHEN DOES THE BASTARD GO ON THE PSYCHIC HOTLINE AND START RAKING IN SERIOUS MONEY?

WHAT THE HELL DOES IT MEAN, ALEX?

TWO HOMELESS MEN, A PSYCHOLOGIST, A WAITER. WIDE RANGE OF AGES, BOTH SEXES, BLACKS, WHITES.

IF THERE'S A CONNECTION, I DON'T SEE IT.

MAYBE WENDELL PELLEY'S BEHIND SOME OF IT. BUT HE DIDN'T DO DADA.

IF DADA'S PART OF THE MIX, IT MEANS MORE THAN ONE KILLER. SAME IF THE BEATTY BROTHERS WERE KILLED SIMULTANEOUSLY.

GREAT, SO THERE'S A PSYCHO ARMY OUT THERE. FOR ALL WE KNOW, PEAKE SPOUTED OFF ABOUT RICHARD, TOO, BUT NO ONE WAS AROUND TO LISTEN.

THE QUESTION IS HOW THE HELL DOES PEAKE KNOW?

HE'S GOT TO HAVE SOME LINK TO THE OUTSIDE, AND PELLEY IS THE ONLY THING THAT FITS.

YOU DON'T BUY IT, DO YOU?

ALL FOUR MURDERS WERE PLANNED. **METICULOUS.** WHOEVER KILLED RICHARD AND CLAIRE KNEW ENOUGH NOT TO STEAL THEIR CARS. MURDERING THE BEATTYS ON THE SAME NIGHT ADDS **MORE** CALCULATION.

I **STILL** THINK IT'S ABOUT PEAKE. HIS CRIMES...THOSE **CLIPPINGS** CLAIRE HELD ON TO. SHE TARGETED HIM BECAUSE THERE WAS SOMETHING SHE WANTED TO LEARN ABOUT HIM. OR **FROM** HIM.

I KEEP THINKING ABOUT **TREADWAY**...THE SCENE OF HIS CRIMES. A FAMILY AND A TOWN WIPED OFF THE MAP. MAYBE THERE'S STILL SOMEONE AROUND THERE WHO REMEMBERS THOSE DAYS.

RIGHT **NOW** BEING THOROUGH MEANS FINDING WENDELL PELLEY.

I JUST DON'T HAVE THE TIME, ALEX. BUT IF **YOU** WANT TO GO OUT THERE, **FINE.**

I'M BEING A CRANKY **BASTARD,** AREN'T I? SORRY. NOT ENOUGH SLEEP, TOO MUCH FUTILITY.

THANKS FOR ALL YOUR TIME ON THIS.

LESS RAW MEAT NEXT TIME. CHECK.

YOU CAN THANK ME WITH A LESS GRUESOME CASE NEXT TIME OUT. A NICE, CLEAN SHOOTING, MAYBE?

I MADE THE TRIP THE NEXT DAY, STOPPING AT THE LIBRARY ON THE WAY TO DIG INTO THE AREA'S HISTORY.

I FOUND SEVERAL ARTICLES ABOUT HENRY "BUTCH" ARDULLO, SCOTT'S FATHER. MERCIFULLY, HENRY HAD DIED NEARLY A DECADE BEFORE THE SLAUGHTER OF HIS SON AND GRANDCHILDREN.

BEFORE THAT, HENRY HAD BEEN AN OUTSPOKEN CRITIC OF FARMERS IN TREADWAY SELLING OUT TO DEVELOPERS. "THE FARM IS THE SOUL OF CALIFORNIA," HE'D SAID.

IT HAD TAKEN THE RAMPAGE OF A MADMAN TO BRING HENRY ARDULLO'S NIGHTMARE HOME.

A FAMILY OBLITERATED. AN ENTIRE TOWN WIPED OFF THE MAP. ONCE SENTIMENTALITY HAD BEEN TAKEN CARE OF, HIGH REAL ESTATE VALUES DID THE REST.

DR. DELAWARE. GOT YOUR MESSAGE.

JACOB HAAS.

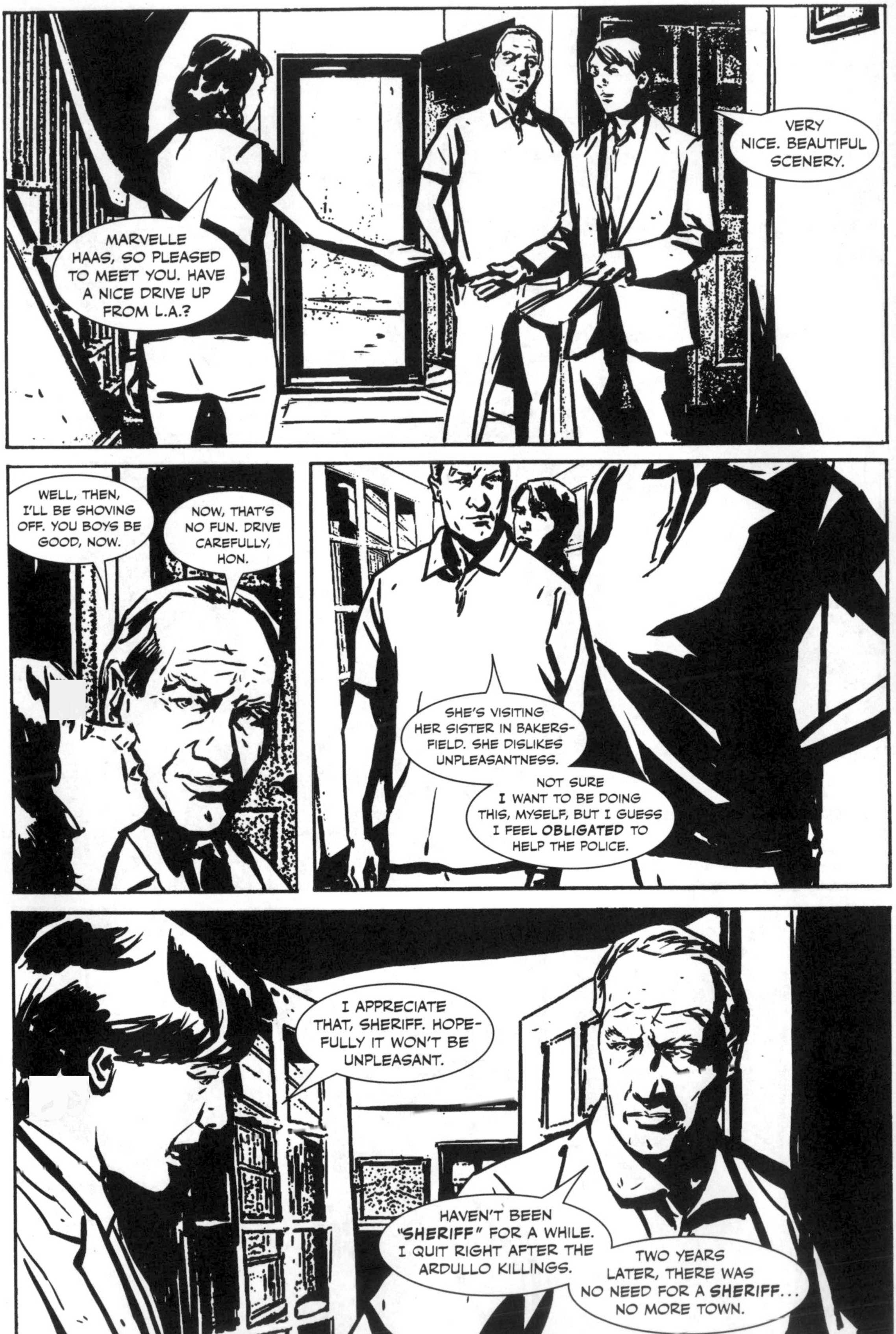
MARVELLE HAAS, SO PLEASED TO MEET YOU. HAVE A NICE DRIVE UP FROM L.A.?
VERY NICE. BEAUTIFUL SCENERY.
WELL, THEN, I'LL BE SHOVING OFF. YOU BOYS BE GOOD, NOW.
NOW, THAT'S NO FUN. DRIVE CAREFULLY, HON.
SHE'S VISITING HER SISTER IN BAKERS-FIELD. SHE DISLIKES UNPLEASANTNESS.
NOT SURE I WANT TO BE DOING THIS, MYSELF, BUT I GUESS I FEEL **OBLIGATED** TO HELP THE POLICE.
I APPRECIATE THAT, SHERIFF. HOPE-FULLY IT WON'T BE UNPLEASANT.
HAVEN'T BEEN **"SHERIFF"** FOR A WHILE. I QUIT RIGHT AFTER THE ARDULLO KILLINGS.
TWO YEARS LATER, THERE WAS NO NEED FOR A **SHERIFF**... NO MORE TOWN.

WAS THERE ANY **RESISTANCE** TO THE BUYOUT AND DEVELOPMENT?

NO. FARMING'S A TOUGH LIFE. IN TREADWAY ONLY **TWO** FAMILIES MADE A GOOD LIVING FROM IT, THE ARDULLOS AND THE CRIMMINSES.

ONCE **THEY** SOLD OUT, IT WAS OVER.

A DERRICK CRIMMINS WAS QUOTED IN AN ARTICLE I READ ABOUT THE CRIME.

CARSON'S SON. THE **YOUNGER** ONE. THERE WERE **TWO** BOYS, DERRICK AND CARSON JUNIOR.

I REMEMBER THEM HANGING AROUND THE CRIME SCENE. MAKES SENSE IF DERRICK TALKED TO THE PRESS...ALWAYS HAD A MOUTH ON HIM.

SO WHY DID THE POLICE SEND A **PSYCHOLOGIST** TO TALK ABOUT THE MONSTER?

DON'T TELL ME THEY'RE THINKING OF LETTING HIM OUT.

NO. HE'S LOCKED UP **TIGHT**. HE'S PRETTY DETERIORATED. ALL BUT CATATONIC.

WELL THAT'S GOOD. HE SHOULDN'T BE **ALIVE**.

THE VILLAGE IDIOT, THAT'S HOW EVERYONE SAW HIM. HE WAS TREATED WITH KINDNESS...PITY, HIM **AND** HIS MOTHER.

SCOTT AND TERRI TOOK THEM IN. GOOD FAMILY, THE ARDULLOS. RICH, BUT DOWN TO EARTH, DESPITE THAT HOUSE BUTCH BUILT. THREE STORIES, WITH A BIG PORCH AND LAND IN ALL DIRECTIONS.

THE CRIMMINS PLACE WAS **JUST** AS BIG, ON THE OTHER SIDE OF THE VALLEY.

YOU **STILL** HAVEN'T TOLD ME WHY YOU'RE HERE.

I BEGAN WITH CLAIRE'S MURDER. HER NAME DREW NO LOOK OF RECOGNITION. I CONTINUED, TELLING HAAS ABOUT PEAKE'S RAMBLINGS.

I CAN'T **BELIEVE** YOU CAME ALL THE WAY UP HERE BECAUSE OF THAT.

RIGHT NOW, THERE'S VERY LITTLE **ELSE** TO GO ON. I KNOW IT'S DIFFICULT, BUT ANYTHING YOU CAN TELL ME ABOUT THAT NIGHT...

I WAS STILL IN BED, THE SUN HAD JUST COME UP WHEN THE CALL CAME.

SOON AS I GOT THERE I COULD TELL SOMETHING WAS WRONG. **REALLY** WRONG. THE LIGHTS WERE ON WHEREVER... LIKE HE WAS SHOWING OFF WHAT HE'D DONE. THE BLOOD LED RIGHT BACK TO HIS SHACK.

THE FBI INTERVIEWED ME. JUST GET YOUR BOSSES AT LAPD TO FIND YOU A COPY.

YOU'RE DIGGING A DRY HOLE, DOCTOR. WHY DON'T YOU GO BACK TO L.A. AND TELL YOUR BOSSES TO FORGET ALL THIS. PEAKE'S LOCKED UP, THAT'S THE MAIN THING.

JUST A FEW MORE THINGS. YOU FOUND PEAKE SLEEPING?

LIKE A...I WAS GOING TO SAY LIKE A BABY. CHRIST.

HE WAS OUT FOR SURE. GOD KNOWS WHAT HE WAS ON. THERE WERE BOOZE BOTTLES, PAINT CANS, ALL KINDS OF PILLS.

AFTER I SAW THE HOT PLATE...WHAT HE'D DONE...IT WAS ALL I COULD DO NOT TO SHOOT HIM RIGHT THERE. IT WAS...

NO. I WON'T GO THERE AGAIN. TOOK ME TOO DAMN LONG TO ERASE THOSE MEMORIES.

MR. HAAS, ANY IDEA WHERE DERRICK CRIMMINS—

GONE, LIKE EVERYONE ELSE. CARSON SENIOR AND HIS SECOND WIFE MOVED TO FLORIDA.

DO YOU REMEMBER HER NAME?

NO. THAT'S ENOUGH, DOCTOR. GOOD BYE. JUST... GOOD BYE.

7

ON MY WAY OUT OF THE VALLEY THAT HAD ONCE BEEN TREADWAY, I TRIPLED THE SPEED LIMIT, UNSURE THAT I'D ACCOMPLISHED ANYTHING MORE THAN RAISING SOMEONE ELSE'S STRESS LEVEL. SOME PSYCHOLOGIST.

HAAS HAD REACTED WITH SPECIAL VEHEMENCE WHEN THE TOPIC WAS THE SECOND MRS. CRIMMINS. WHY?

I STOPPED TO MAKE SOME CALLS, LEARNED THAT THE TREADWAY TOWN RECORDS HAD ENDED UP AT A PUBLIC LIBRARY IN BAKERSFIELD.

HERE YOU GO...TWENTY YEARS OF THE TREADWAY *INTELLIGENCER*. YOU'RE IN LUCK. IT WAS A WEEKLY.

I SETTLED IN FOR THE LONG HAUL.

THE EDITOR-IN-CHIEF WAS A MAN NAMED ORTON HATZLER, THE MANAGING EDITOR WANDA HATZLER. I COPIED DOWN *BOTH* NAMES AND STARTED TO READ.

WEATHER REPORTS ON THE FRONT PAGE, BECAUSE EVEN IN CALIFORNIA WEATHER MATTERED TO FARMERS.

BUTCH ARDULLO'S NAME POPPED UP *FREQUENTLY*, MOSTLY IN STORIES RELATED TO HIS LEADERSHIP IN THE LOCAL FARM ORGANIZATION.

CARSON CRIMMINS'S NAME SHOWED UP REGULARLY, TOO. THE OTHER RICH MAN IN TOWN. NO PICTURES OF HIM.

CRIMMINS HAD STARTED OUT AS BUTCH ARDULLO'S ALLY IN THE FIGHT FOR THE FAMILY FARM, BUT HAD SWITCHED COURSE AT SOME POINT, ADVERTISING HIS WILLINGNESS TO SELL "TO THE HIGHEST SERIOUS BIDDER."

MARCH 1975. THE **DEATH** OF BUTCH ARDULLO. TWO EXTRA PAGES IN A MEMORIAL ISSUE.

CARSON CRIMMINS SAID, "WE HAD OUR DIFFERENCES, BUT HE WAS A MAN'S MAN."

JUNE 1976. ANNOUNCEMENT OF CRIMMINS'S MARRIAGE TO "THE FORMER SYBIL NOONAN, A THESPIAN WHO MET MR. C. ON A CRUISE TO THE BAHAMAS."

CRIMMINS'S GRIN WAS PAINFUL, ESPECIALLY IN CONTRAST TO THE THOUSAND-WATT SMILE OF HIS BRIDE. TRUE **LOVE**, PERHAPS THE **ROCK** ON HER FINGER HAD SOMETHING TO DO WITH IT?

THE CRIMMINS BOYS: CARSON, JR. AND DERRICK. BOTH WERE THIN, RANGY, WITH PROMINENT NOSES AND A TOUCH OF THEIR FATHER'S AVIAN LOOK.

BETTER-LOOKING THAN THEIR FATHER... STRONGER CHINS, BROADER SHOULDERS. BOTH PROJECTED THAT IMMOVABLE SULLENNESS UNIQUE TO TEENAGERS AND MUG-SHOT CRIMINALS.

FOR YEARS, NO MENTION OF LAND SALES. CRIMMINS'S HOPED-FOR DEAL FALLING THROUGH BECAUSE SCOTT ARDULLO HAD REFUSED TO SELL AND NO ONE WANTED HALF A LOAF?

NOTHING OF INTEREST TILL JANUARY 5, 1980, "THE FARM LEAGUE NEW YEAR'S BALL". SCOTT ARDULLO DANCING, BUT **NOT** WITH HIS **WIFE**. IN HIS ARMS WAS SYBIL CRIMMINS, WHITE-BLOND HAIR LONG AND FLOWING OVER BARE TAN SHOULDERS.

HE LOOKED DOWN AT HER, SHE GAZED UP AT HIM. SOMETHING IN HIS EYES AT ODDS WITH THE SOLID-YOUNG-BUSINESSMAN IMAGE. TOO MUCH HEAT AND LIGHT. DOPEY SURRENDER.

WAS THIS WHY JACOB HAAS HAD TIGHTENED UP WHEN TALKING ABOUT SYBIL CRIMMINS? SCOTT, A BOY HE'D LONG ADMIRED, STRAYING WITH A PLATINUM-HAIRED STRUMPET FROM L.A.?

THE PICTURE SEEMED TO GIVE OFF WAVES OF HEAT. I WAS SURPRISED THE INTELLIGENCER HAD PUBLISHED IT.

THREE WEEKS LATER, ORTON AND WANDA HATZLER'S NAMES WERE GONE FROM THE PAPER'S MASTHEAD.

SYBIL CRIMMINS TOOK OVER. SHE COVERED THE "SLAUGHTER AT THE ARUDLLO RANCH," IN AN EDITORIAL, "HOW COULD THIS HAPPEN HERE...IN TREADWAY?!" THAT WAS THE LAST EDITION OF THE INTELLIGENCER.

I RETURNED THE CART AND MOVED TO THE MAIN REFERENCE DESK. A COMPUTER DATABASE SEARCH FOR "CRIMMINS" RETURNED A FEW RESULTS.

I TRACKED DOWN THE CORRESPONDING ARTICLES ON MICROFICHE. CARSON AND SYBIL HAD DIED TWELVE YEARS AGO, IN A YACHT EXPLOSION OFF THE COAST OF SOUTH FLORIDA.

CARSON, JR. WAS KILLED IN VEGAS. A MOTOCROSS ACCIDENT. NOTHING ON THE YOUNGER BROTHER, DERRICK.

STILL NOT MUCH TO GO ON, BUT SOMETHING ABOUT PEAKE'S CRIMES HAD CAUGHT CLAIRE'S INTEREST, AND NOW SHE WAS DEAD, ALONG WITH THREE OTHERS, AND PEAKE HAD PREDICTED TWO OF THE MURDERS. THERE HAD TO BE A COMMON THREAD.

I WONDERED ABOUT WANDA HATZLER. ANOTHER SEARCH FOUND A NUMBER IN SANTA MONICA. HOPING SHE COULD HELP CONNECT SOME OF THE DOTS, I HEADED TO A PAY PHONE.

DR. DELAWARE? WANDA HATZLER. I LIKE YOUR CAR.

WE USED TO HAVE A FLEETWOOD UNTIL ORTON COULDN'T DRIVE ANYMORE.

SOMETHING TO **DRINK**? COKE, DIET COKE, **RUM**? I WAS JUST GOING TO HAVE SOME SOUP.

I'M FINE, THANKS.

TOUGH CUSTOMER. **TREADWAY**, HUH? WHAT A HOLE. WHY ON EARTH WOULD YOU WANT TO KNOW ANYTHING ABOUT IT?

I TOLD HER ABOUT CLAIRE AND PEAKE, KEEPING PROPHECY OUT OF IT, OMITTING THE OTHER MURDERS.

I'M AFRAID I CAN'T GIVE YOU ANY IDEAS ON PEAKE. NEVER HAD A FEEL FOR HIM.

TOO BAD. YOU'RE GOOD-LOOKING AND I WAS LOOKING FORWARD TO THIS.

TREADWAY WAS THE LAST STOP FOR ORTON'S DREAM OF BEING A JOURNALIST. GAWD, I **HATED** THAT PLACE.

STUPID PEOPLE...SOCIAL DARWINISM, I SUPPOSE. THE SMART ONES LEAVE, AND ONLY THE IDIOTS ARE LEFT TO BREED.

THE ONLY REASON I STAYED THERE WAS BECAUSE I LOVED THE GUY. HE WAS EVEN HANDSOMER THAN YOU. VIRILE, TOO.

WERE THOSE EYELASHES BATTING?

THE ARDULLOS AND THE CRIMMINSES. THEY WERE AT ODDS ON THE LAND DEALS?

SURE. GOD, BUTCH AND CARSON RAN THAT DUMP LIKE A FIEFDOM.

WHAT DID YOU THINK OF THE SECOND WIFE, SYBIL?

SLUT. GOLD DIGGER. DUMB BLONDE, RIGHT OUT OF A BAD MOVIE.

CLAIMED TO BE AN ACTRESS. RIGHT, AND I'M THE SULTAN OF BRUNEI.

I SAW A PICTURE OF HER AND SCOTT ARDULLO AT A DANCE.

WE MIGHT AS WELL HAVE PUBLISHED THEM NAKED. ORTON WOULDN'T HAVE PRINTED IT, BUT HE WAS SLOSHED THAT DAY.

EVERYONE IN TOWN KNEW, ANYWAY. PEOPLE KNOW EVERYTHING ABOUT EACH OTHER IN SUCH A SMALL TOWN.

CARSON KNEW, I'M SURE. HE WAS MUCH OLDER. MAYBE HE COULDN'T CUT THE MUSTARD?

MY, THIS IS GREAT FUN.

WHAT ABOUT THE CRIMMINS BOYS?

OBNOXIOUS... SPOILED ROTTEN. CARSON GAVE THEM FAST CARS, WHICH THEY RACED DOWN MAIN STREET.

IT WAS COMMON KNOWLEDGE THAT THEY DRANK AND TOOK DRUGS. LUCKY THEY NEVER KILLED ANYONE.

THEY TREATED THE MIGRANTS LIKE DIRT. I REMEMBER ONE NIGHT...

"I'D JUST FINISHED WITH THE PAPER, WALKED OUTSIDE TO GET SOME AIR, WHEN A CAR SCREECHED TO A STOP."

"I KNEW RIGHT AWAY WHOSE IT WAS."

"THE BACK DOOR OPENED, SOMEONE FELL OUT, AND THE CAR SPED AWAY."

"THIS LITTLE MEXICAN GIRL...SHE COULDN'T HAVE BEEN OLDER THAN FIFTEEN. SHE SPOKE NO ENGLISH. I TRIED TO TALK TO HER, BUT SHE RAN AWAY."

"I KNEW WHAT THOSE LITTLE SHITS HAD DONE, AND I KNEW THERE'D BE NO CONSEQUENCES. NOT FOR THE CRIMMINS BOYS."

HOW DID THEY GET ALONG WITH THEIR STEP-MOTHER—

ARE YOU ASKING IF THEY **SLEPT** WITH HER?

ACTUALLY, MY IMAGINATION HADN'T CARRIED ME **THAT** FAR.

WHY NOT? DON'T YOU WATCH TALK SHOWS?

TO BE FAIR, I NEVER PICKED UP AN INKLING OF ANY-THING **QUITE** SO REPELLENT.

SHE DID MANAGE TO GET DERRICK INVOLVED WITH THOSE RIDICULOUS THEATER PRODUCTIONS SHE PUT ON.

IF YOU FIND THE LITTLE SHIT, I'M SURE HE'LL BE **HAPPY** TO RIDICULE PEAKE. HE AND HIS BROTHER DELIGHTED IN TORMENT-ING ARDIS.

SPEAKING OF PEAKE, ANY **THEORIES** ABOUT WHY HE KILLED THE ARDULLOS?

HE WAS CRAZY. **YOU'RE** THE PSYCHOLOGIST. WHY DO CRAZY PEOPLE ACT CRAZY?

I'VE TAKEN ENOUGH OF YOUR TIME. YOU'VE BEEN VERY HELPFUL.

OH, **PLEASE,** NONE OF THAT.

LONGEVITY CAN BE HELL, DOCTOR. LIVE LONG ENOUGH AND YOU **KNOW** THINGS WILL INEVITABLY GO BAD. YOU JUST DON'T KNOW WHEN.

I LEFT WANDA'S HOUSE, MY HEAD STUFFED WITH HISTORY AND HINTS.

MORE HATRED AND INTRIGUE IN TREADWAY THAN I'D COUNTED ON. STILL NO CONNECTION TO CLAIRE ARGENT.

I WAS WIPED OUT, BUT MY SERVICE HAD A CALL FROM MILO. I DROVE TO THE STATION, ASKED FOR HIM AT THE DESK, AND WAITED.

SO, WHEN ARE YOU BUYING A LOT ON LAKE TREADWAY?

NOT IN THIS LIFE. WHAT'S THE NEWS FROM COP CENTRAL?

NOTHING ON PELLEY YET. THE BEATTY TWINS HAVE BEEN OCCUPYING MY DAY.

BROTHER LEROY TOLD HIS FELLOW JUICEHEADS THAT HE HAD AN ACTING GIG AWHILE BACK.

HE SHOWED UP A WEEK LATER, STILL PENNILESS. HIS BUDDIES FIGURED HE'D FLUSHED IT DOWN HIS GULLET.

OR MAYBE MR. GRIFFITH D. WARK STIFFED SOMEONE ELSE.

STILL NOTHING ON ELLROY, THE LONER TWIN. LIVED BY HIMSELF NEAR THE TRAIN TRACKS.

SO, BACK TO THE MOVIE ANGLE. MAYBE A LINK BETWEEN RICHARD DADA AND THE TWINS, BUT STILL NO TIE-IN WITH CLAIRE, EXCEPT SHE WENT TO MOVIES.

AND, WHY WOULD WARK BUMP OFF HIS CAST?

MAYBE HE'S FILMING MURDER.

OR A VARIANT... NOT **NECESSARILY** A SEXUAL ANGLE.

A CHRONOLOGY OF UNNATURAL DEATH...A LITERAL BLOOD WALK.

SNUFF MOVIES?

THAT WOULD **EXPLAIN** WHY THE SCRIPT'S NEVER BEEN REGISTERED AND WHY WARK USED A FAKE NAME TO GET HIS EQUIPMENT.

IT COULD ALSO EXPLAIN THE DIVERSITY OF VICTIMS AND METHODS.

HE MIGHT SEE HIMSELF AS A SPLATTER **AUTEUR.** PLAYING GOD BY SETTING UP CHARACTERS—REAL PEOPLE—THEN BUMPING THEM OFF.

PSYCHOPATHS DEPERSONALIZE THEIR VICTIMS. THIS IS THE **ULTIMATE** DEGRADATION: REDUCING HIS "CAST" TO PROTOTYPES: THE TWINS, THE ACTOR.

AS FOR PEAKE, HE COULD BE INVOLVED BECAUSE WARK **WANTS** HIM INVOLVED. BECAUSE WARK'S SOMEONE OUT OF PEAKE'S PAST. AND I'VE GOT A POSSIBLE **CANDIDATE** FOR WARK: DERRICK CRIMMINS.

I TOLD HIM WHAT I'D LEARNED ABOUT TREADWAY. THE CONFLICT BETWEEN THE ARDULLOS AND THE CRIMMINSES, SCOTT'S AFFAIR WITH SYBIL, THE CRIMMINS BOYS' ANTISOCIAL BEHAVIOR, DERRICK'S INVOLVEMENT WITH SYBIL'S ABORTIVE THEATER GROUP.

DERRICK MATCHES THE PHYSICAL DESCRIPTION VITO BONNER GAVE US OF WARK, AND HIS AGE FITS.

SO ALL THE CRIMMINSES EXCEPT THIS DERRICK ARE DEAD?

FATHER, STEP-MOTHER, BROTHER, ALL BY ACCIDENTAL DEATH. INTERESTING, ISN'T IT?

WANDA HATZLER DESCRIBED DERRICK AND HIS BROTHER AS BRUTAL BULLIES. WHAT IF THEY WERE PEAKE'S DRUG SUPPLIERS, TOO?

PEAKE GOT MASSIVELY STONED AND SNAPPED. SOMEONE ELSE MIGHT BE HORRIFIED BY THAT, BUT THE CRIMMINS BOYS HAD PLENTY OF REASON TO HATE SCOTT.

HE WAS SLEEPING WITH THEIR STEP-MOM.

WHAT IF THEY WERE PLEASED WITH WHAT PEAKE HAD DONE?

ALL RIGHT. I'LL TRY TO LOCATE HIM. MEANWHILE, WHOEVER WARK IS, HOW'S HE CONTACTING PEAKE?

AND, IN A SICK SENSE, IT ALL WORKED OUT FOR THEM. THE LAND DEAL WENT THROUGH, THE FAMILY BECAME RICH AGAIN.

DERRICK LEARNS HOW FUN AND PROFITABLE MURDER CAN BE.

MAYBE HE WORKS AT STARK-WEATHER.

GREAT. SO, I GET TO TALK TO MY OLD PAL SWING AGAIN.

CHRIST, ALEX. IF ONLY YOU WERE A STUPID GUY AND I COULD KISS OFF YOUR FANTASIES.

THE NEXT MORNING ROBIN AND I STAYED IN FOR BREAKFAST.

FOR NEARLY AN HOUR THOUGHTS OF CLAIRE ARGENT AND ARDIS PEAKE WERE PUSHED TO THE BACK OF MY MIND.

THE PHONE RANG AS WE WERE NURSING CUPS OF COFFEE. MARY HERTZLINGER AGAIN.

"DR. DELAWARE, I'M SORRY TO CALL YOU AT HOME."

NO PROBLEM. DID SOMETHING **NEW** COME TO MIND?

"WELL, NOT **EXACTLY.** MORE LIKE SOMETHING NEW CAME TO **LIGHT.**"

"I RAN INTO EILEEN RACANO. SHE USED TO WORK WITH US...CLAIRE AND I. NICE LADY. SHE'S MOVED ON NOW, TOO."

"SHE'D LEARNED SOMETHING WHEN CLAIRE WAS HIRED...SOMETHING SHE'D KEPT TO HERSELF, OUT OF COURTESY."

"EILEEN ONLY FOUND OUT BY ACCIDENT. SHE WAS—SORRY. I'M RAMBLING."

"THE POINT IS, CLAIRE HAD KNOWN SOMEONE LIKE PEAKE **BEFORE** SHE GOT TO STARKWEATHER."

I FOUND THE *DETAILS* IN THE RESEARCH LIBRARY NEWSPAPER FILES. THE PITTSBURGH POST-GAZETTE, TWENTY-SEVEN YEARS AGO.

IT COULD HAVE BEEN *ANY* MAJOR PAPER. THE STORY HAD BEEN COVERED NATIONALLY. FOUR DEAD...TWO PARENTS AND TWO KIDS.

THE WEAPONS HAD BEEN A KNIFE AND A TENDERIZING MALLET FROM THE KITCHEN.

THEY'D FOUND THE KILLER CROUCHED IN THE BASEMENT, STILL CLUTCHING THE MURDER WEAPONS AND DRENCHED IN BLOOD.

DENTON RAY ARGENT, 19. CLAIRE'S OLDER *BROTHER*. FIVE YEARS LATER, HE WOULD DIE IN THE ASYLUM HE'D BEEN COMMITTED TO. A BRAIN SEIZURE.

IT EXPLAINED SO MUCH. I'D WONDERED ABOUT FAMILY CHAOS, BUT MY IMAGINATION HADN'T STRETCHED FAR ENOUGH. CLAIRE PUNISHING HERSELF, TRYING TO *BOND* SOMEHOW WITH THE BROTHER WHO'D POLLUTED HER FORMATIVE YEARS.

THE PARALLELS BETWEEN THE TWO CASES CHILLED MY BLOOD. I COULD ONLY IMAGINE HOW CLAIRE HAD FELT WHEN SHE'D DISCOVERED ARDIS PEAKE. CLAIRE'S MOVE TO STARKWEATHER, HER ZEROING IN ON ARDIS PEAKE, WASN'T PUZZLING AT ALL.

SO MANY MADMEN, SO LITTLE TIME. NOT A *CHOICE*, REALLY. A PSYCHOLOGICALLY PREORDAINED DANCE BACKED BY THE CHOREOGRAPHY OF PAIN. A DEAD *CERTAINTY*.

NO LUCK ON THE CORVETTE OR ON ANY SORT OF *LOCALE* ON WARK OR DERRICK CRIMMINS.

CORVETTE?

YEAH. I SPOKE TO THE MAITRE D' WHERE RICHARD DADA WAS WORKING HIS WAITER GIG.

ONE CUSTOMER OF RICHARD'S STOOD OUT. WAIT FOR IT...TALL, THIN WHITE GUY WHO MAYBE WORE A WIG. DROVE A YELLOW CORVETTE, SEVENTIES VINTAGE.

SO FAR IT AMOUNTS TO EXACTLY *ZILCH.* OH, AND...WENDELL PELLEY IS NO LONGER A SUSPECT, AT LEAST NOT FOR THE BEATTYS.

HE'S BEEN DEAD FOR OVER A WEEK...*BEFORE* CHOO CHOO BANG BANG.

HIS BODY SHOWED UP IN A COUNTY GARBAGE DUMP SIX DAYS AGO.

NO SIGN OF *VIOLENCE* TO THE CORPSE. PROBABLY FELL ASLEEP IN THE DUMPSTER AND GOT SHIPPED OUT WITH THE TRASH.

CAUSE OF DEATH WAS EXTREME DEHYDRATION AND MAL-NUTRITION. SONOFABITCH *STARVED* HIMSELF.

NO WOUNDS. THE ONLY DAMAGE WAS WHAT THE *MAG-GOTS* HAD DONE.

HE COULD STILL BE GOOD FOR CLAIRE.

IF I COULD SHOW THAT HE AND CLAIRE EVER MET, MAYBE.

BUT, GIVEN THAT HE'S **NOT** GOOD FOR DADA OR THE BEATTYS, MY ENTHUSIASM FOR HIM HAS FADED CONSIDERABLY.

MAYBE I CAN THROW YOU A LITTLE CHEER. I KNOW **WHY** CLAIRE SOUGHT OUT PEAKE.

I TOLD MILO ABOUT DENTON ARGENT'S RAMPAGE. HIS CHEWING SLOWED.

HER **BROTHER**, HUH? NEVER HEARD OF THE CASE, BUT I WAS IN 'NAM WHEN IT HAPPENED.

SO SHE GETS CLOSE TO PEAKE, TRIES TO GET HIM TO OPEN UP ABOUT WHAT HE DID.

MAYBE SHE DID **MORE** THAN TRY. IF ANYONE COULD PRY HIM OPEN...

WHAT IF SHE SUCCEEDED, AND PEAKE TOLD HER SOMETHING THAT PUT HER IN DANGER? SOMETHING LIKE HE'D BEEN PRODDED BY THE CRIMMINS BROTHERS.

OR, PEAKE'S **STILL** IN CONTACT WITH CRIMMINS AND TOLD HIM CLAIRE WAS GETTING TOO NOSY.

VERY **CREATIVE**, ALEX, BUT IT ALL HINGES ON PEAKE HAVING CONVERSATIONS. HE'S FAKING THE VEG ACT?

MAYBE HIS MENTAL DULLNESS ISN'T ALL **PSYCHOSIS**? WHAT IF IT'S CAUSED BY HIS MEDS?

LET'S SAY CLAIRE DECIDED TO WITHDRAW PILLS IN ORDER TO RESTORE SOME CLARITY. AND IT **WORKED**.

SHE **TAMPERED** ON THE SLY?

SHE HAD INTENSE **MOTIVATION**. IF SHE THOUGHT EASING UP ON HIS THORAZINE WOULD OPEN HIM UP, WHY NOT?

CLAIRE WANTED A WINDOW INTO PEAKE'S VIOLENCE. AND, BY **EXTENSION**, DENTON'S.

WITH CLAIRE GONE, PEAKE GETS HIS FULL DOSAGE AGAIN... BECOMES A BABBLING IDIOT AGAIN.

ALL THIS STILL HINGES ON WARK WORKING AT STARKWEATHER. WE NEED TO TALK TO SWIG.

SOMETHING JUST HIT ME. THE EYE WOUNDS. WHAT'S A **CAMERA LENS**.

ALL-SEEING, INVISIBLE, OMNISCIENT. THE DIRECTOR AS **GOD**. THESE CRIMES ARE ABOUT POWER.

CAMERA OBSERVATION GOES ONLY ONE WAY. I SEE, YOU DON'T. NO EYES FOR YOU.

AN **EYE**.

WE DECIDED TO START OUR STARKWEATHER VISIT WITH CLAIRE'S LIVING SKILLS GROUP. CHET RECOGNIZED US RIGHT AWAY.

YO BRO MY MAN WHUS *SHAKIN* AND *BAKIN* BAKED ALASKA JUNEAU!

YOU KNOW HOT COLD TIGHTASS DON'T *SNEEZE* ON ME HOMEY YOU TOO HOMELY HOMO!

GENTLEMEN...

...THESE GUYS ARE FROM THE PO-LICE.

THEY WANT TO ASK YOU SOME *QUESTIONS* ABOUT DR. ARGENT.

PO-LICE! GOOD MAN GENDARME RIGHT TO BEAR TWO ARMS GOT TO *GUARD* SOCIETY!

I WAS PO-LICE *MYSELF* PO-LITE POE—

THE *JEWS* DID IT.

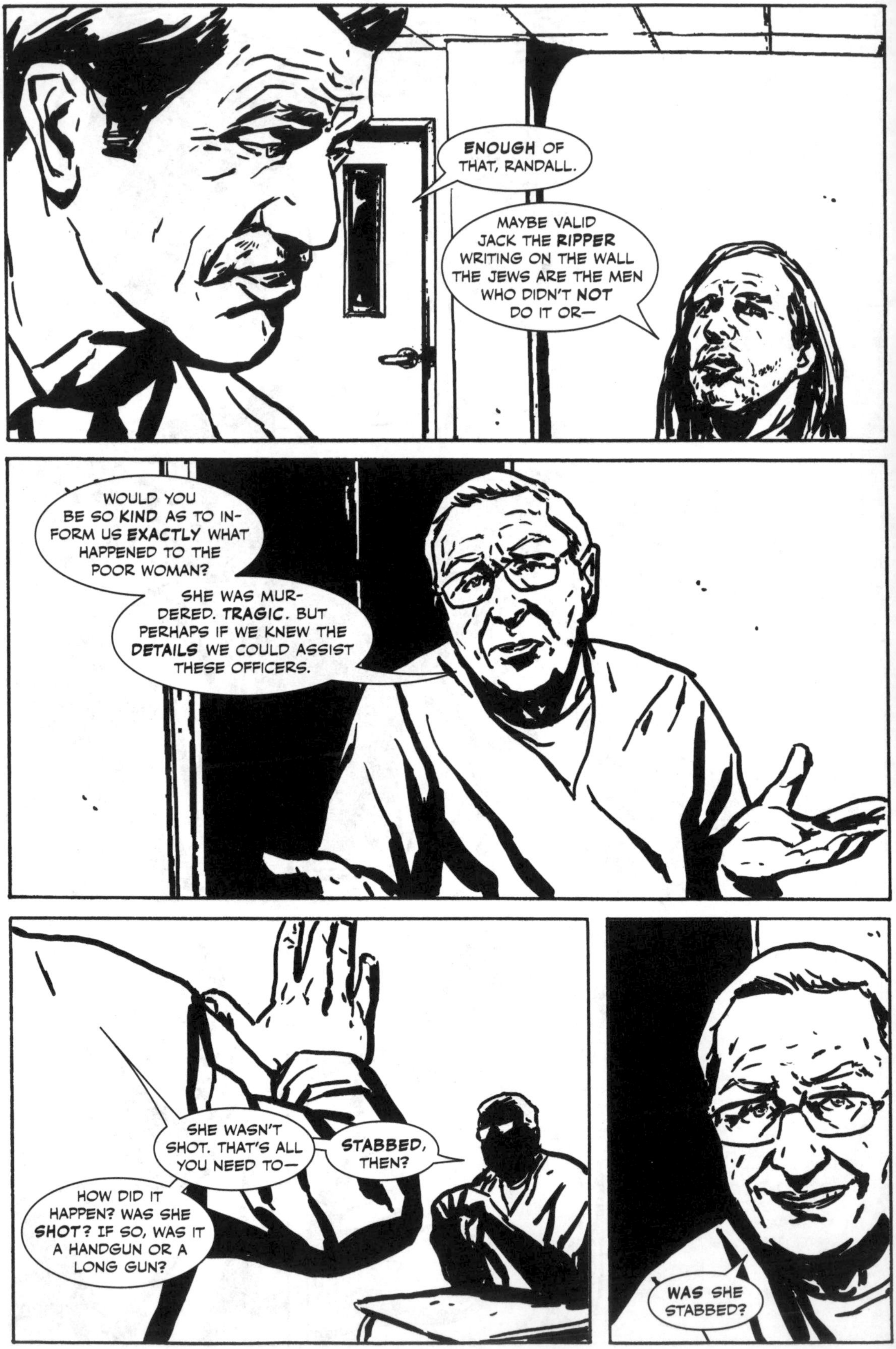
ENOUGH OF THAT, RANDALL.
MAYBE VALID JACK THE RIPPER WRITING ON THE WALL THE JEWS ARE THE MEN WHO DIDN'T NOT DO IT OR—
WOULD YOU BE SO KIND AS TO INFORM US EXACTLY WHAT HAPPENED TO THE POOR WOMAN?
SHE WAS MURDERED. TRAGIC. BUT PERHAPS IF WE KNEW THE DETAILS WE COULD ASSIST THESE OFFICERS.
HOW DID IT HAPPEN? WAS SHE SHOT? IF SO, WAS IT A HANDGUN OR A LONG GUN?
SHE WASN'T SHOT. THAT'S ALL YOU NEED TO—
STABBED, THEN?
WAS SHE STABBED?

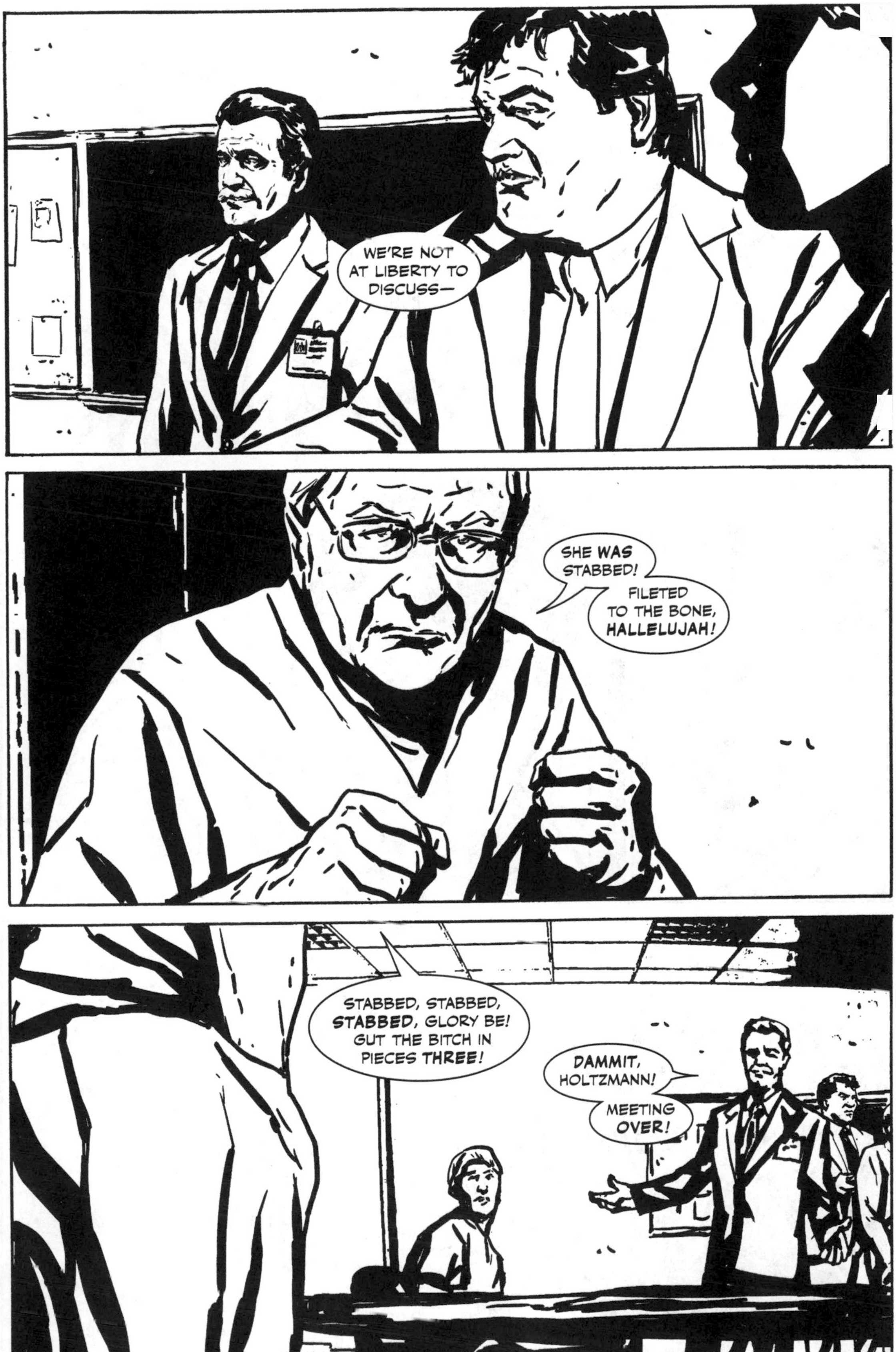
WE'RE NOT AT LIBERTY TO DISCUSS—
SHE WAS STABBED!
FILETED TO THE BONE, HALLELUJAH!
STABBED, STABBED, STABBED, GLORY BE! GUT THE BITCH IN PIECES THREE!
DAMMIT, HOLTZMANN!
MEETING OVER!

WE WAITED IN THE CORRIDOR AS TECHS SWEPT IN TO RESTORE ORDER.

"WHAT THE HELL..."

...ARE YOU TRYING TO ACCOMPLISH?!

IF YOUR REAL GOAL IS TO SOLVE A MURDER, THEN MOVE ON.

YOUR COMING IN HERE IS DISRUPTIVE AND POINTLESS. NO ONE HERE HAD ANYTHING TO DO WITH DR. ARGENT.

BECAUSE NO ONE GETS OUT? WENDELL PELLEY GOT OUT.

A NUTCASE GETS OUT, A FEW WEEKS LATER ONE OF HIS SHRINKS IS DEAD?

DR. ARGENT WAS NEVER ONE OF PELLEY'S SHRINKS.

WHAT DID PELLEY DO TO GET OUT?

MORE LIKE WHAT HE DIDN'T DO. ACT CRAZY. HE HADN'T BEEN CRAZY FOR A LONG TIME.

IN MY OPINION, THE GUY WAS NEVER REALLY PSYCHOTIC, JUST A HORRIBLE DRUNK.

AFTER A MONTH IN HERE, AWAY FROM THE BOOZE, HIS ACTING OUT STOPPED ENTIRELY.

WHY WASN'T HE SENT BACK TO TRIAL?

WHEN HE GOT ARRESTED WE WERE STILL DOING NOT GUILTY BY REASON. HE WAS OFF THE HOOK.

LUCKY HIM.

NOT SO LUCKY. HE STILL GOT COOPED UP HERE FOR TWENTY-ODD YEARS. LONGER THAN HE WOULD'VE BEEN IN PRISON.

WHY? HAS HE CAUSED PROBLEMS ON THE OUTSIDE?

ONLY FOR HIMSELF. STARVED HIMSELF TO DEATH. THEY FOUND HIM IN A GARBAGE DUMP.

HE NEVER DID LIKE TO EAT.

HE WASN'T REALLY THAT BAD OF A GUY. HE WAS SINCERELY REMORSEFUL. DIDN'T EVEN WANNA GET OUT.

I THINK WE'VE WASTED ENOUGH TIME AND TAXPAYER MONEY FOR ONE DAY. TIME TO GO, GENTLEMEN.

I WANT TO SEE PEAKE.

YEAH, AND I WANT TO FUCK SHARON STONE.

TAKE YOU TO PEAKE...WHY? BECAUSE YOU ORDER ME TO?

BECAUSE I CAN BE BACK HERE IN AN HOUR WITH A **WARRANT** ON YOU FOR OBSTRUCTION.

I'M TALKING CENTRAL BOOKING. YOU SAID YOU USED TO BE A COP, SO YOU KNOW THE DRILL.

YOU HAVE **NO** IDEA WHAT KIND OF DEEP SHIT YOU'RE GETTING YOURSELF INTO.

I HAVE A REAL **GOOD** IDEA, FRANK. LET'S PLAY THE MEDIA GAME. BUNCH OF TV CREWS. CAMERAS.

I'LL TELL THEM WE WERE SADDLED WITH A HORRIFIC HOMICIDE AND YOU DID **EVERYTHING** IN YOUR POWER TO IMPEDE US.

MAYBE A SIDEBAR ABOUT THE MASS MURDERER LET OUT WHO PROMPTLY TURNED HIMSELF INTO GARBAGE.

WHY WOULD AN EX-COP BE SO **UNCOOPERATIVE**, FRANK? MAKES ME WONDER IF I SHOULD BE LOOKING CLOSER AT **YOU**.

WHEN'S THE LAST TIME YOU HAD YOUR FINGERS ROLLED FOR PRINTS?

SCREW IT. YOU GET TEN MINUTES WITH PEAKE, IN AND OUT.

NO, FRANK. I **GET** WHAT I **WANT**.

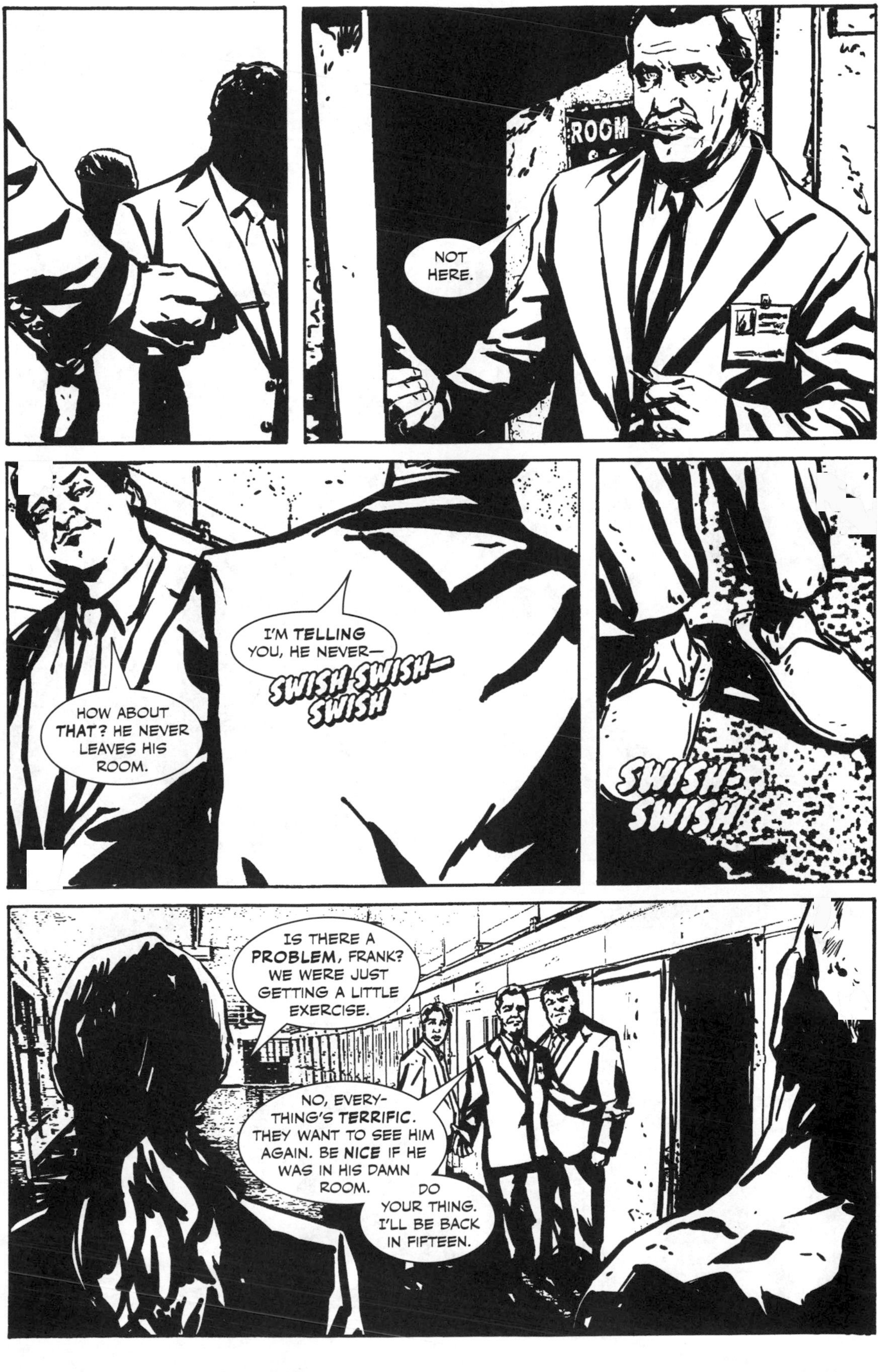

ROOM
NOT HERE.
HOW ABOUT THAT? HE NEVER LEAVES HIS ROOM.
I'M TELLING YOU, HE NEVER—
SWISH-SWISH-SWISH
SWISH-SWISH
IS THERE A PROBLEM, FRANK? WE WERE JUST GETTING A LITTLE EXERCISE.
NO, EVERYTHING'S TERRIFIC. THEY WANT TO SEE HIM AGAIN. BE NICE IF HE WAS IN HIS DAMN ROOM.
DO YOUR THING. I'LL BE BACK IN FIFTEEN.

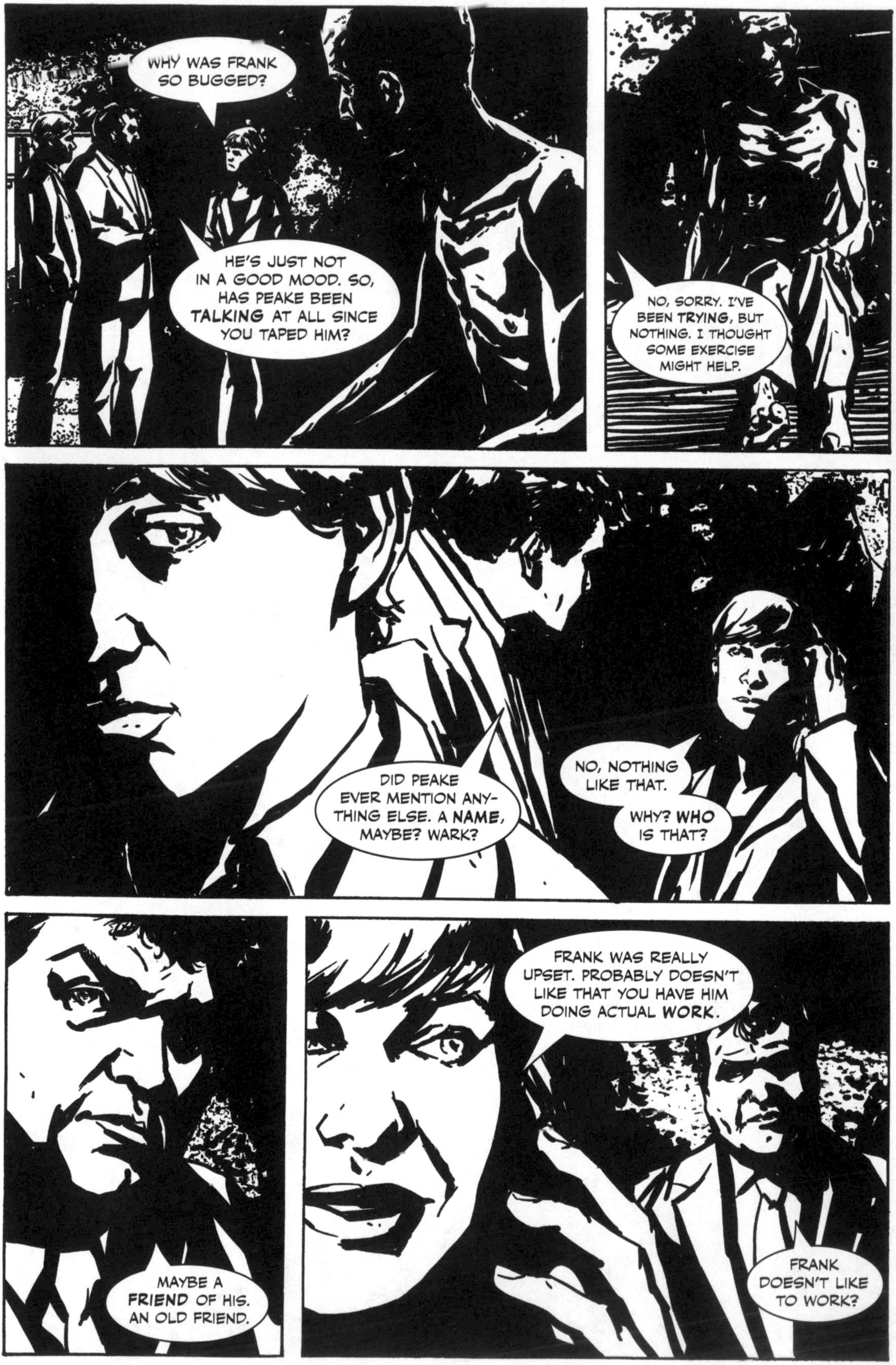
WHY WAS FRANK SO BUGGED?
HE'S JUST NOT IN A GOOD MOOD. SO, HAS PEAKE BEEN TALKING AT ALL SINCE YOU TAPED HIM?
NO, SORRY. I'VE BEEN TRYING, BUT NOTHING. I THOUGHT SOME EXERCISE MIGHT HELP.
DID PEAKE EVER MENTION ANY-THING ELSE. A NAME, MAYBE? WARK?
NO, NOTHING LIKE THAT.
WHY? WHO IS THAT?
MAYBE A FRIEND OF HIS. AN OLD FRIEND.
FRANK WAS REALLY UPSET. PROBABLY DOESN'T LIKE THAT YOU HAVE HIM DOING ACTUAL WORK.
FRANK DOESN'T LIKE TO WORK?

I HEARD HE GOT **FIRED** FROM SOME POLICE DEPARTMENT FOR SLEEPING ON THE JOB.

SWIG LIKES HIM, SO HE DOESN'T **ACTUALLY** HAVE TO DO TOO MUCH.

WHAT'S THIS WARK DONE?

PROBABLY NOTHING, JUST WORKING ALL THE ANGLES.

YOU DRILL A BUNCH OF WELLS, HOPE FOR A **TRICKLE** EVERY NOW AND THEN.

HEIDI, WE VISITED THE LIVING SKILLS GROUP. IT'S HARD TO UNDERSTAND WHY CLAIRE PICKED SUCH LOW-FUNCTIONING MEN.

WE KNOW ABOUT CHET, BUT CAN YOU TELL US ANYTHING ABOUT THE **REST**? WHY THEY'RE HERE?

LET'S SEE, THERE'S EZZARD **JACKSON**...SKINNY BLACK GUY. HE KILLED HIS WIFE. TIED HER UP IN THEIR HOUSE AND BURNED IT DOWN.

SAME WITH **HOLTZMANN**, THE OLD MAN. HE CUT HIS WIFE UP, STORED THE PIECES IN THE FREEZER, MARKED THEM THE WAY A BUTCHER WOULD...FLANK, LOIN.

RANDALL SHOT HIS PARENTS. HE WAS INTO SOME NAZI STUFF, HAD SOME DELUSION THEY WERE PART OF A ZIONIST PLOT.

I LISTENED TO THE LITANY OF **HORRORS**, CONNECTING EACH TO THE MEN WE'D OBSERVED. "SO MANY MADMEN, SO LITTLE TIME..."

ALL EXCEPT CHET VICTIMIZED **FAMILY** MEMBERS.

ACTUALLY, CHET WASN'T **PICKED** FOR THE GROUP. HE FOUND OUT ABOUT IT, ASKED CLAIRE IF HE COULD JOIN.

YEAH, YOU'RE **RIGHT.** I NEVER THOUGHT ABOUT IT, BUT SHE MUST'VE BEEN **INTERESTED** IN FAMILY KILLERS.

YOU'LL KEEP WORKING WITH PEAKE?

I **GUESS,** IF YOU WANT ME TO. I'M READY TO MOVE ON FROM THIS PLACE.

I WAS KIND OF WAITING UNTIL YOU GOT TO THE BOTTOM OF CLAIRE'S MURDER.

WISH I COULD TELL YOU IT WOULD BE SOON, HEIDI. MEAN-WHILE, AS LONG AS DR. DELAWARE'S HERE...

"...HE MIGHT AS WELL GIVE PEAKE A TRY."

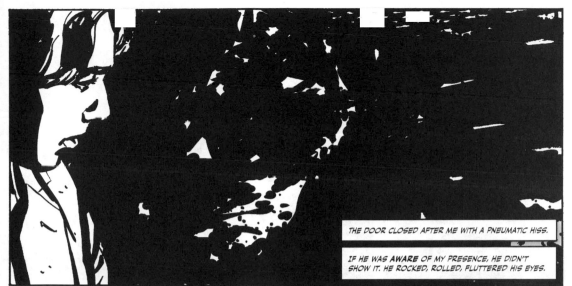

THE DOOR CLOSED AFTER ME WITH A PNEUMATIC HISS.

IF HE WAS **AWARE** OF MY PRESENCE, HE DIDN'T SHOW IT. HE ROCKED, ROLLED, FLUTTERED HIS EYES.

MY NOSE HABITUATED TO THE STINK.

KEEPING MY EYES ON PEAKE'S HANDS, I EDGED CLOSER. I BEGAN TO DETECT A **CADENCE** TO HIS MOVEMENTS.

TONGUE-THRUST, CURL AND HOVER, LINGUAL RETREAT, NECK ROLL CLOCK-WISE, THEN COUNTERCLOCKWISE.

TEN-SECOND **SEQUENCES.**

HIS HANDS RESTED ON RUMPLED, SWEAT-STAINED COVERS. HANDS THAT HAD WREAKED SO MUCH **RUIN**...

I HEARD A TAPPING FROM BELOW. TWO THIN FEET, **DRUMMING** THE FLOOR.

SO MUCH **MOTION**, BUT NO FLAVOR OF **INTENT**...THE INANIMATE DANGLE OF A PUPPET.

ARDIS.

I LEANED IN CLOSER. HAD HE WANTED TO KISS ME OR CLAW OUT MY EYES, HE COULD'VE.

ARDIS, THIS IS DR. DELAWARE. I WANT TO TALK TO YOU ABOUT DR. ARGENT.

ANOTHER TIC...A JERKY WAVE TRAVELING BENEATH THE PAPERY SKIN.

DEFINITE RESPONSE. ON SOME LEVEL, HE WAS ABLE TO FOCUS.

YOU WERE IMPORTANT TO DR. ARGENT.

SHE WAS IMPORTANT TO YOU, ARDIS. TELL ME WHY.

WATCHING HIM NOW, THE NOTION OF THIS HUSK DECAPITATING HIS OWN MOTHER, INFLICTING ALL THE AGONY AND DEATH, SEEMED REMOTE.

AS UNLIKELY AS KINDLY MR. HOLTZMANN SECTIONING AND FREEZING HIS WIFE. IN THIS PLACE, LOGIC MEANT NOTHING.

KNOWING THIS MIGHT BE MY LAST SHOT, I DECIDED TO KEEP GOING. I MOVED IN CLOSE ENOUGH TO WHISPER.

DR. ARGENT. CLAIRE ARGENT.

THE EYES OPENED AND I RETREATED WITH A POUNDING HEART. WAS HE *SEEING* ME?

THE BEATTY BROTHERS. THE ARDULLOS...SCOTT. TERRI.

THE EYES WERE ALIVE NOW. FIXED ON MINE. AWAKE. CLEAR INTENT. TO DO WHAT?

"SCOTT AND TERRI ARDULLO. SCOTT AND TERRI. BRITTANY AND JUSTIN."

THE EYES. METRONOMIC, HYPNOTIC. I FELT MYSELF BEING DRAWN IN. AVOID THAT, WATCH HIS HANDS...

DID HIS ARM JUST *MOVE?* FEAR STABBED ME AND I BACKED AWAY. HE DIDN'T SEEM TO NOTICE.

HE WAS UNSTEADY, BUT MANAGED TO KEEP HIMSELF UPRIGHT. STRONGER THAN HE'D APPEARED BEFORE.

HE *STARED*. STRAIGHTENED HIS SPINE, STEPPING *TOWARD* ME.

A SHRILL, DRY SOUND ESCAPED FROM HIS MOUTH. SOFT, WISPY, BUT IT POUNDED MY EARS.

OKAY, YOU'VE **DONE** IT, DELAWARE. **SUCCESS!** NOW WHAT?

HOW MUCH **DAMAGE** COULD HE DO, UNARMED, SO FEEBLE? STILL, I BRACED MYSELF, PLOTTED MY DEFENSE.

EYES STRETCHED OPEN. I COULD SEE WET PINK BORDERS ALL AROUND.

TEARS WELLING, OVERFLOWING, STREAMING DOWN SUNKEN CHEEKS.

POSING NOW...AN UNMISTAKABLE POSE.

WEEPING JESUS. HE STAYED THAT WAY. JUST...*STAYED* THAT WAY.

THE NAMES OF HIS VICTIMS HAD LOOSENED HIS TEARS. REMORSE OR SELF-PITY? OR SOMETHING I COULD NEVER *HOPE* TO UNDERSTAND? MARTYR POSE. NO REMORSE AT ALL? SEEING HIMSELF AS A VICTIM?

SUDDENLY, THE ABSURDITY AND FUTILITY OF WHAT I WAS DOING HIT ME... TRYING TO PRY INFORMATION FROM A DISEASED MIND THAT SMOOTHLY MORPHED SIN AND SALVATION. HAD *CLAIRE* PRODDED PEAKE THE SAME WAY? DIED, SOMEHOW, BECAUSE OF HER CURIOSITY?

HIS HEAD ROTATED, LIFTED A BIT. FACED ME. SOMETHING SURFACED IN HIS EYES THAT I HADN'T SEEN BEFORE.

SHARPNESS. *CLARITY* OF PURPOSE. HE NODDED. *KNOWINGLY.* AS IF THE TWO OF US SHARED SOMETHING. I PRESSED MY BACK AGAINST THE DOOR

THE SPACE OPENED BEHIND ME AND I TUMBLED BACK.

I TOLD THEM HOW THE NAMES OF THE VICTIMS HAD *TRIGGERED* THE POSING.

HAS HE DONE THIS *BEFORE*, HEIDI?

NO. NEVER. HE NEVER GETS OFF THE BED.

WHAT'D YOU *SAY* TO WORK HIM UP LIKE THAT?

NOTHING. JUST THE *NAMES*, LIKE I SAID.

BULLSHIT. YOU PEOPLE KEEP COMING IN HERE, DISRUPTING, GOING AT PEAKE.

LOOK AT *THAT*. GUY LIKE THAT, WHO *KNOWS* WHAT COULD HAPPEN? AND FOR WHAT?

IT'S NOT *MEANINGLESS*, FRANK.

HE SHOWED AFFECTIVE *RESPONSE*.

HE WAS CRYING.

DOLLARD LED US TO THE GATE, SLAMMED IT AFTER US WITHOUT A WORD.

I LET THE CAR IDLE AND CRANKED THE A/C. MILO CALLED POLICE DEPARTMENTS UNTIL HE FOUND WHERE FRANK DOLLARD USED TO WORK.

HE HUNG UP, LOOKING LIKE HE'D SWALLOWED SOMETHING SLIMY.

HEIDI WAS RIGHT.

DOLLARD WAS A MAJOR-LEAGUE GOLDBRICK: LAZY, TOOK UN-AUTHORIZED LEAVES, THE WORKS.

SWIG LIKES HIM. TELLS YOU SOME-THING ABOUT SWIG.

THEY FINALLY CONVINCED HIM TO MOVE ALONG FOUR YEARS AGO, AND HE CAME HERE.

PERFECT FOR FRANK. THE NUTCASES DON'T COMPLAIN WHEN HE SLACKS OFF.

I'D BEEN THINKING OF PEAKE AS LETHAR-GIC, STUPOROUS, BUT HE CAN MOVE FAST WHEN HE WANTS TO.

IF HE'D JUMPED ME, I'D HAVE BEEN UN-PREPARED.

SO HE'S NOT A TOTAL VEG. MAYBE HE'S A SNEAKY BASTARD, PLAYING ALL OF US.

MAKES SENSE WHEN YOU THINK ABOUT HOW HE WALKED IN ON HIS MOTHER.

SHE'S SITTING THERE CORING APPLES, HE GETS BEHIND HER WITH THAT KNIFE...

SO, WAS HE CRYING REAL TEARS?

CUPIOUSLY. BUT I'M NOT SURE IT WAS REMORSE. IT FELT LIKE SOMETHING ELSE... SELF-PITY.

THE JESUS POSE FITS THAT, TOO. AS IF HE SEES HIMSELF AS A MARTYR.

SICK BASTARD.

OR MAYBE HEARING THE KIDS' NAMES EVOKED AN OVERPOWERING MEMORY.

RECALL OF NOT ACTING ALONE. OF SOMETHING THE CRIMMINS BOYS PUT HIM UP TO.

MAYBE HE COMMUNICATED THAT TO CLAIRE. IF SHE LOWERED HIS DOSAGE...

WHY DO YOU THINK DOLLARD TURNED SO HOSTILE? SOMETHING TO HIDE?

WHAT ABOUT SOME KIND OF HOSPITAL SCAM? MAYBE TRAFFICKING IN PRESCRIPTION DRUGS.

CLAIRE FOUND OUT ABOUT IT AND THAT'S WHAT PUT HER IN JEOPARDY. MAYBE PEAKE KNEW, TOO. HE KNEW SOMEONE WAS GOING TO HURT CLAIRE. THE "PROPHECY" WAS HIS WAY OF WARNING HER.

CLAIRE WASN'T AT WORK THAT DAY, SO PEAKE DID THE NEXT BEST THING...TOLD HER ASSISTANT.

IF WARK IS DERRICK CRIMMINS, HIS WORKING THERE MAKES SENSE ON ANOTHER LEVEL. HE WAS **DRAWN** BY PEAKE'S PRESENCE, JUST AS CLAIRE WAS.

PEAKE'S RAMPAGE MADE A MAJOR IMPRESSION ON HIM.

AND IF MY GUESS ABOUT HIS BEING PEAKE'S DRUG SOURCE IN THE PAST IS RIGHT, THAT FITS WITH THE RACKET BEING A DOPE THING.

DOLLARD SMUGGLES OUT PHARMACEUTICALS, **WARK** SELLS THEM ON THE STREET.

BEING THE OUTSIDE MAN **ALSO** MAKES WARK THE PERFECT CHOICE FOR AMBUSHING AND MURDERING CLAIRE.

IT'LL TAKE A COURT ORDER TO GET ACCESS TO THE PERSONNEL RECORDS.

WE DON'T HAVE ENOUGH FOR THAT.

HOW ABOUT APPROACHING IT ANOTHER WAY? IMPERSONATING A DOC- TOR IS TOO **RISKY**. A WOULD-BE PRODUCER DOWN ON HIS LUCK MIGHT SEE CUSTODIAL WORK AS BENEATH HIM.

PSYCHIATRIC TECHNICIAN, ON THE OTHER HAND, HAS SOME **CACHET**. PSYCH TECHS ARE LICENSED BY THE STATE.

THE MEDICAL BOARD KEEPS A ROSTER.

IF WARK SEES HIMSELF AS SOME DARK-SIDE CINEMA *AUTEUR*, WHAT BETTER PLACE TO DREDGE UP BLOODY PLOTS THAN STARKWEATHER?

THAT COULD EXPLAIN RICHARD AND THE BEATTY TWINS: THEY'RE PART OF WARK'S FILM GAME.

NOT BAD. WORTH A TRY.

THE SNUFF EXTRAVAGANZA, AGAIN. JESUS, WE'RE ALL OVER THE PLACE WITH THIS.

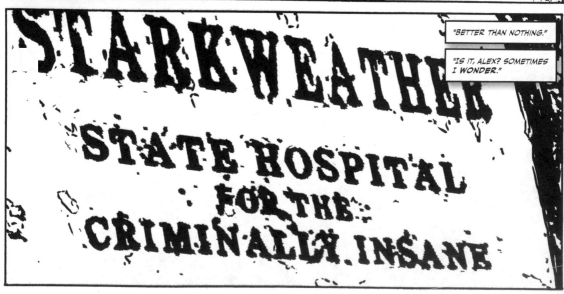

"BETTER THAN NOTHING."

"IS IT, ALEX? SOMETIMES I WONDER."

STARKWEATHER

STATE HOSPITAL FOR THE CRIMINALLY INSANE

WE RETREATED TO MILO'S OFFICE TO MAKE CALLS. HE REACHED OUT TO A RETIRED DETECTIVE IN FLORIDA, WHILE I TRIED PSYCHIATRIC LICENSING BUREAUCRATS.

A SUPERVISOR AGREED TO FAX A LIST THAT FIT THE TIME FRAME FOR WARK TO BE AT STARKWEATHER WITH CLAIRE.

NO WARK. I LOOKED FOR OTHER ITERATIONS OF AUTEUR DIRECTORS' NAMES.

I'D JUST FOUND SOMETHING WHEN MILO HUNG UP HIS LINE.

TALKED TO A COP NAMED CASTRO. HE WORKED THE DEATHS OF OLD MAN CRIMMINS AND HIS WIFE.

HE'S BEEN WAITING FOR SOMEONE TO CALL ABOUT OUR BOY DERRICK.

SEEMS SOME-ONE STRAPPED A PIPE BOMB TO THE FUEL TANK OF THE FAMILY BOAT.

BOOM. NOT MUCH LEFT BUT SOME SHREDS OF BONE.

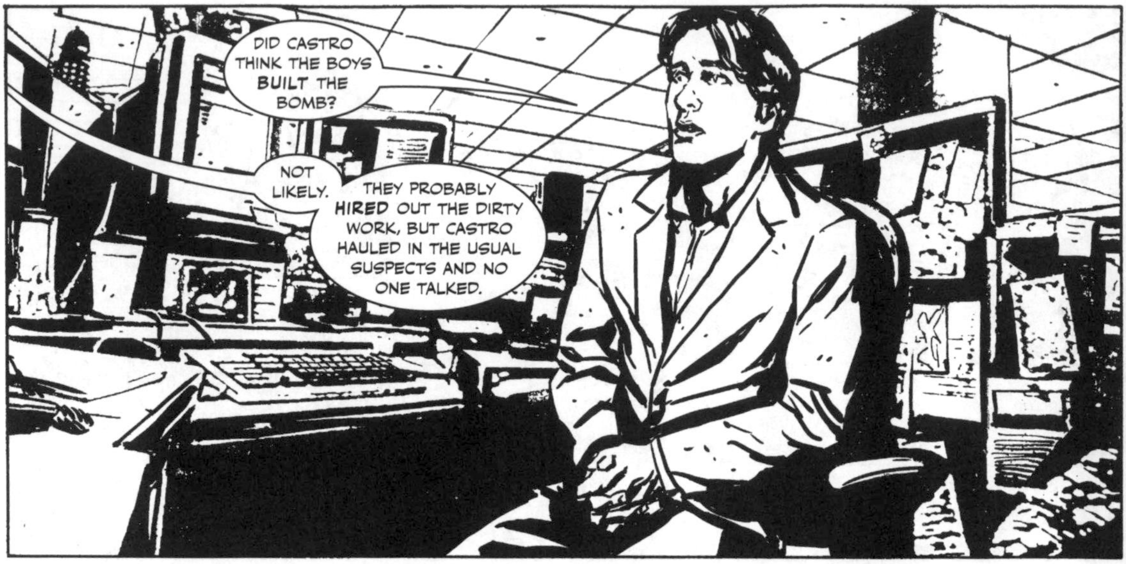
DID CASTRO THINK THE BOYS BUILT THE BOMB?
NOT LIKELY.
THEY PROBABLY HIRED OUT THE DIRTY WORK, BUT CASTRO HAULED IN THE USUAL SUSPECTS AND NO ONE TALKED.

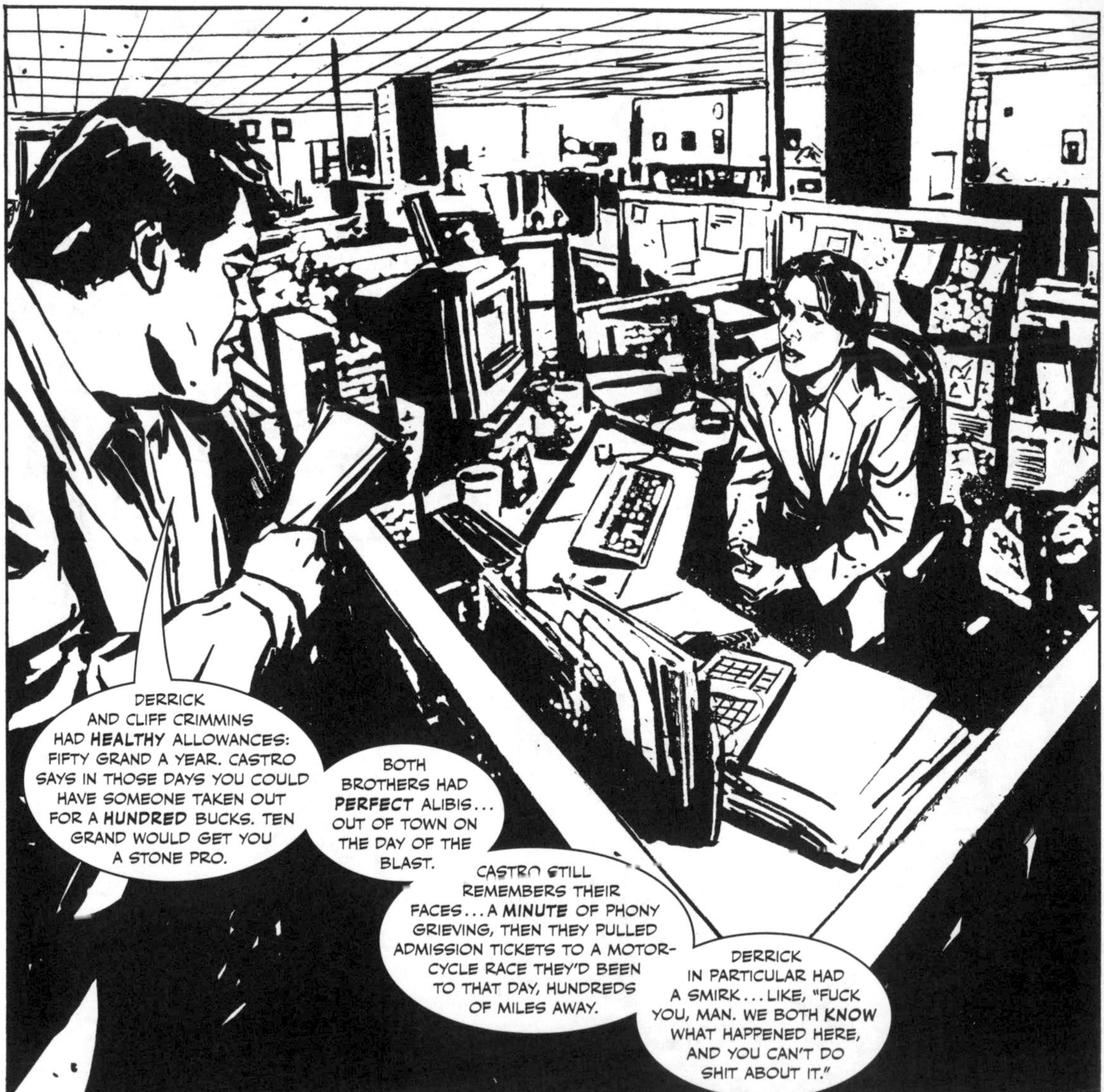
DERRICK AND CLIFF CRIMMINS HAD HEALTHY ALLOWANCES: FIFTY GRAND A YEAR. CASTRO SAYS IN THOSE DAYS YOU COULD HAVE SOMEONE TAKEN OUT FOR A HUNDRED BUCKS. TEN GRAND WOULD GET YOU A STONE PRO.
BOTH BROTHERS HAD PERFECT ALIBIS... OUT OF TOWN ON THE DAY OF THE BLAST.
CASTRO STILL REMEMBERS THEIR FACES... A MINUTE OF PHONY GRIEVING, THEN THEY PULLED ADMISSION TICKETS TO A MOTOR-CYCLE RACE THEY'D BEEN TO THAT DAY, HUNDREDS OF MILES AWAY.
DERRICK IN PARTICULAR HAD A SMIRK... LIKE, "FUCK YOU, MAN. WE BOTH KNOW WHAT HAPPENED HERE, AND YOU CAN'T DO SHIT ABOUT IT."

IT WASN'T THE CRIMMINS BOYS' **FIRST** BRUSH WITH THE LAW, EITHER.

THEY'D BEEN RUNNING **SCAMS**...PICKING UP SENILE OLD FOLKS AT THE BEACH AND DRIVING THEM OUT TO SOME **BOGUS** VACATION LOTS.

SMALL-TIME CRAP...FIVE OR SIX HUNDRED BUCKS A POP, FOR "DOWN PAYMENTS."

THEY GOT **BUSTED** WHEN THEY PICKED ON THE WRONG MARK...THE MOTHER OF A LOCAL DOCTOR.

THEY SERVE **TIME?**

NEVER CHARGED. DADDY HIRED A SLICK **LAWYER,** AND ALL THE WITNESSES WERE OLD. I.D.S WOULD HAVE BEEN SHAKY.

THE BROTHERS WORE **DISGUISES:** WIGS, FAKE MUSTACHES, GLASSES. AMATEUR SHIT, BUT IT WAS **ENOUGH.**

PAPA CRIMMINS MADE **RESTITUTION,** AND THE WHOLE THING WENT AWAY.

SO...DERRICK HAS A LONG **HISTORY** OF PLAY-ACTING.

YEAH. I CAUGHT THAT, TOO.

YOU MENTION CLIFF'S **DEATH** BY **MOTOCROSS** TO CASTRO?

OH, YEAH. DERRICK ALWAYS **WAS** THE IDEA GUY, AND THEY BOTH HAD LOTS OF BIKES.

HE WOULD HAVE **KNOWN** HOW TO RIG ONE.

CASTRO'S **STILL** PISSED ABOUT THE CRIMMINS BOYS SKATING.

HE SAID THE ONLY **COMFORT** WAS THAT THEY DIDN'T GET AS **RICH** OUT OF KILLING DADDY AS THEY'D EXPECTED.

TURNS OUT THE OLD MAN WAS IN **DEBT** UP TO HIS EARS. THE KIDS ONLY CLEARED ABOUT EIGHTY GRAND EACH.

OH, AND THE KICKER WAS THE **BOAT**. CRIMMINS OWNED THAT FREE AND CLEAR, AND THE LITTLE SHITS BLEW IT **UP**.

SO...**FIRST** DERRICK KILLS HIS PARENTS, **THEN** HIS BROTHER, PROBABLY JUST FOR HIS SHARE OF THE HUNDRED AND SIXTY GRAND.

THAT'S **PROFESSIONAL** EVIL.

DERRICK THE DOMINATOR. ARROGANT, LIKE YOU'VE BEEN SAYING.

GOOD CRIMINAL SELF-ESTEEM, AND WHY **NOT**? HE DOES HORRIFIC THINGS AND GETS AWAY CLEAN.

AND, MAYBE HE HAD EARLIER **PRAC-TICE** WITH FAMILY ELIMINATION.

THE **ARDULLOS**? SPURRING PEAKE ON? WELL, YOUR GUESSES HAVE BEEN PRETTY RIGHT ON SO FAR.

MEANWHILE, THE GUY'S RIGHT HERE, POLLUTING MY CITY, AND I CAN'T PUT A FINGER ON HIM.

PSYCHIATRIC TECH LICENSES ARE GRANTED FOR PERIODS RANGING FROM THIRTEEN TO TWENTY-FOUR MONTHS.

THESE ARE THE NAMES THAT FIT OUR TIME-LINE. NO CRIMMINS, NO WARK...SO, I STARTED WONDERING ABOUT *OTHER* ALIASES. DERRICK IS ARROGANT, BUT STRANGELY CHILDLIKE, PLAYING PRETEND GAMES.

SEES HIMSELF AS A MAJOR HOLLYWOOD **PLAYER**. OF COURSE, HE'S NEVER ACTUALLY PRODUCED ANYTHING, BUT HELL...YOU COULD SAY THE **SAME** FOR HALF OF THE SLUGS AT SPAGO'S.

SO, WHAT DID *YOUR* PHONE WORK NET US?

I LOOKED FOR *OTHER* AUTEURS: HITCHCOCK, WELLES, HUSTON, FORD. NOTHING, BUT WARK WAS GRIFFITH'S **MIDDLE** NAME, SO... A CALL TO THE UNIVERSITY REFERENCE LIBRARY FOR FULL NAMES.

ALFRED JOSEPH HITCHCOCK, GEORGE ORSON WELLES AND SO ON. BACK TO THE LIST, AND GUESS WHAT?

WANT TO GO CHECK OUT THE LAST KNOWN **ADDRESS** OF MR. G.W. ORSON?

WE RAN THEORIES ON THE WAY.

IF ORSON AND WARK WERE BOTH CRIMMINS' ALIASES, MAYBE HE'D RUN INTO CLAIRE AT STARKWEATHER.

THEY HAD *TWO* COMMON INTERESTS: ARDIS PEAKE AND MOVIES. MAYBE HE'D CAST HER IN BLOOD WORK.

HAVE YOU SEEN
BUDDY
$100 **REWARD**

BUDDY LOOKED STRANGELY *FAMILIAR* TO ME. THE SWIRLING NATURE OF THE CASE....*EVERYTHING* WAS STARTING TO REMIND ME OF SOMETHING.

EMPTY. I'D SAY IT HAS BEEN FOR A WHILE.

WANT TO CALL THE OWNER?

MAYBE LATER. THERE ARE *LIGHTS* ON NEXT DOOR...

GO AWAY

NOK-NOK

"...LET'S TRY THE NEIGHBOR FIRST."

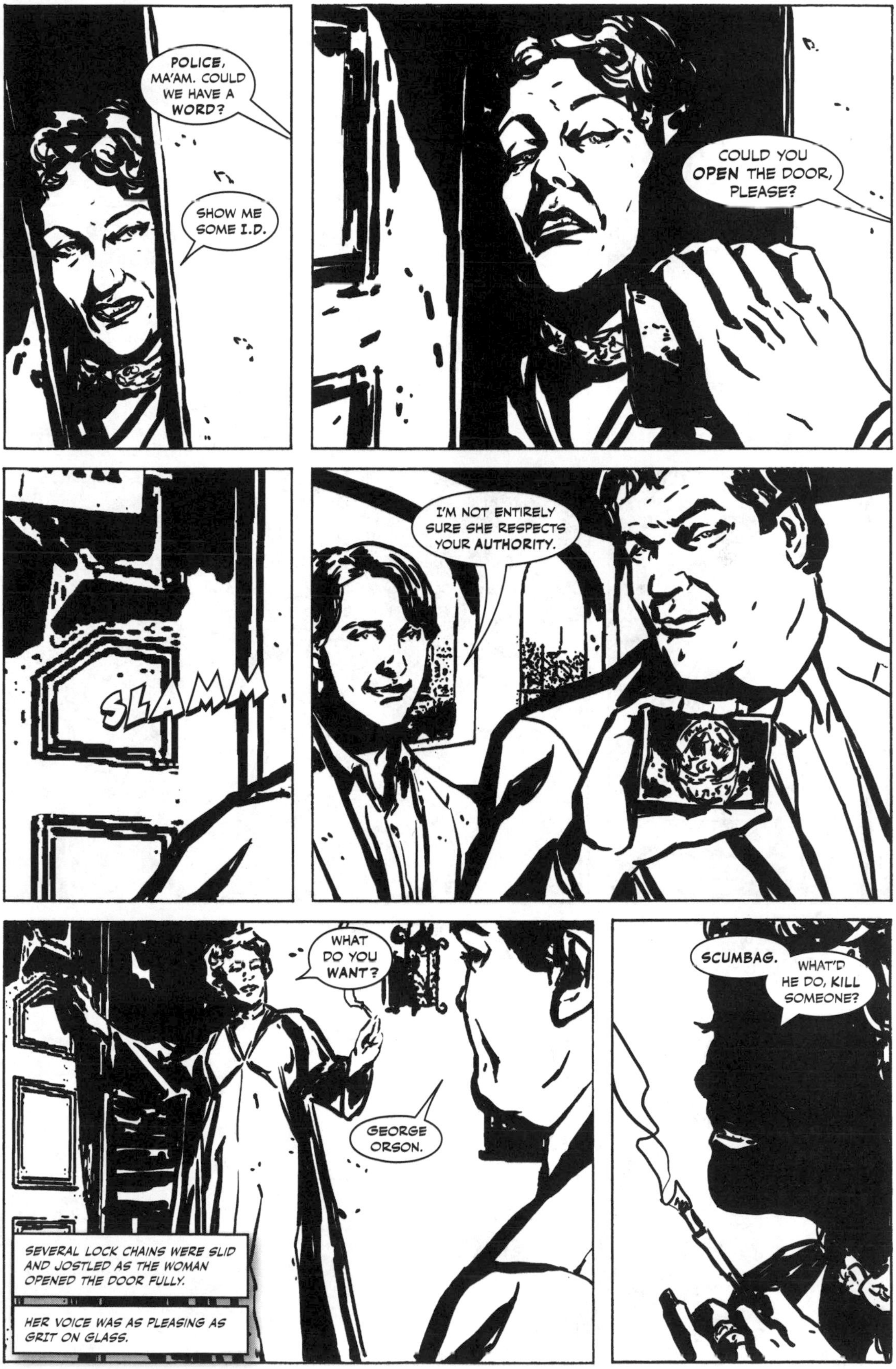
POLICE, MA'AM. COULD WE HAVE A WORD?
SHOW ME SOME I.D.
COULD YOU OPEN THE DOOR, PLEASE?
SLAMM
I'M NOT ENTIRELY SURE SHE RESPECTS YOUR AUTHORITY.
WHAT DO YOU WANT?
GEORGE ORSON.
SEVERAL LOCK CHAINS WERE SLID AND JOSTLED AS THE WOMAN OPENED THE DOOR FULLY.
HER VOICE WAS AS PLEASING AS GRIT ON GLASS.
SCUMBAG.
WHAT'D HE DO, KILL SOMEONE?

MR. ORSON IS **SUSPECTED** IN SOME DRUG THEFTS.

THAT'S WHAT WE'RE **TRYING** TO FIND OUT, MRS.—

MS. SINCLAIR. MS. MARIE SINCLAIR, AND IF YOU WANT INFO FROM ME, CUT THE **CRAP.**

WHAT. DID. HE. DO?

BIG FREAKING **SURPRISE.** I ONLY CALLED ABOUT HIM SIX TIMES. YOUR SO-CALLED **OFFICERS** SAID THEY'D DRIVE BY.

HORSESHIT.

CARS **COMING** AND **GOING** AT ALL HOURS.

HOW THE HELL WAS I SUPPOSED TO **PRACTICE** WITH ALL THAT GOING ON?

PRACTICE **WHAT,** MA'AM?

PIANO. I GIVE RECITALS...USED TO DO RADIO WORK.

I KNEW OSCAR LEVANT...ANOTHER DRUG FIEND. **BRILLIANT,** BUT A **LUNATIC.**

YOU PRACTICE AT **NIGHT,** MA'AM?

THAT AGAINST THE **LAW?** I'M A NIGHT PERSON. COMES FROM MY YEARS PLAYING CLUBS.

NIGHTTIME'S WHEN IT COMES **ALIVE.** MORNING PEOPLE SHOULD BE LINED UP AND **SHOT.**

HOW MANY **CARS** ARE WE TALKING ABOUT, MS. SINCLAIR?

FIVE, SIX, TEN PER NIGHT...I NEVER COUNTED.

AT LEAST HE WAS **GONE** A LOT. THANK GOD FOR SMALL BLESSINGS.

"THAT **GARAGE**...DOES IT BELONG TO YOU OR WAS IT ORSON'S?"

SUPPOSED TO BE MINE, BUT I WOULDN'T KEEP ANYTHING OF VALUE THERE. NOT IN **THIS** NEIGHBORHOOD.

THAT **SCUMBAG** USED IT. NOT THAT HE EVER ASKED.

HAD SOME KIND OF WORK-SHOP BACK THERE.

LOOK FOR YOURSELVES IF YOU LIKE. THINK HE WAS MAKING **DOPE** BACK THERE?

ANYTHING'S **POSSIBLE**, MA'AM. JUST ONE MORE THING...

...THIS WOMAN. EVER SEE **HER** WITH ORSON?

NOPE. LOOKS LIKE A SCHOOL-TEACHER.

THAT SONOFA-BITCH **KILLED** HER, DIDN'T HE?

119

SNIFF-SNIFF

DISINFECTANT.

SOMEONE **CLEANED** THIS OUT PRETTY WELL.

YEAH. MAYBE THEY **MISSED** SOMETHING.

IT TOOK AN HOUR TO GET A CRIMINOLOGIST TEAM TO THE GARAGE. IN **ANOTHER** HOUR, THEY HAD PRELIMINARY RESULTS.

PRETTY DE-GRADED, DETECTIVE. NOT SURE ABOUT DNA, BUT WE CAN TRY.

DEFINITELY BLOOD, THOUGH. O-POSITIVE.

RICHARD DADA'S TYPE.

MILO DROVE ME HOME. ROBIN AND I SETTLED IN FOR A **PEACEFUL** NIGHT, WITH ME TRYING TO PUSH THOUGHTS OF GEORGE ORSON/DERRICK CRIMMINS TO THE BACKGROUND.

A FEW HOURS AFTER HE'D DROPPED ME OFF, MILO CALLED. HE'D BEEN CHASING PAPER, WITH SOME **RESULTS**.

TAX REFUNDS SHOWED GEORGE ORSON'S **LAST** PLACE OF EMPLOYMENT: STARKWEATHER.

AND... SWIG HAD CALLED, THIS TIME WITH AN **INVITATION**.

AN **IMMEDIATE** INVITATION, AND SOMETHING **ELSE** I HADN'T SHARED WITH ROBIN...

...MILO SAID HE SOUNDED SCARED.

THE GUARD HAD WAVED US THROUGH THE GATE, WITHOUT EVEN ASKING MILO TO SURRENDER HIS GUN.

I ASKED MILO WHAT HE THOUGHT OF THE RED CARPET TREATMENT.

DUNNO. THIS IS ALL TOO EASY.

I **HATE** IT WHEN THINGS ARE TOO EASY.

GATE

THE TECH USHERED US THROUGH EMPTY CORRIDORS WITHOUT A WORD...TOWARD PEAKE'S ROOM.

MILO HADN'T *EXAGGERATED.* THE FEAR WAS WRITTEN ACROSS SWIG'S PALE FACE.

THANK YOU FOR COMING.

IT'S... JUST SEE FOR YOURSELVES.

PEAKE'S ROOM, BUT NO *PEAKE.* JUST A *BODY,* LYING WHERE ARDIS HAD PLAYED JESUS ON THE CROSS.

DOLLARD. WHEN?

WHAT A SHOCK. I SUPPOSE YOU DID ME A FAVOR CALLING ME AT ALL.

SOMEONE FOUND HIM TWO **HOURS** AGO.

WE HAD TO CONDUCT OUR **OWN** INVESTIGATION...LOOK FOR PEAKE.

WE... WE HAVEN'T **FOUND** HIM.

LOOKS LIKE ONE CUT **ACROSS** THE THROAT. HAS ANYONE MOVED HIM?

NO. NOTHING'S BEEN **TOUCHED**.

ALL RIGHT. LET'S **CLEAR** THE ROOM, AND GIVE ME YOUR KEY.

MILO LOCKED THE ROOM AND CALLED THE SHERIFF'S OFFICE.

WHEN WE'D COME IN THE PLACE HAD BEEN QUIET. NOW THE SILENCE FALTERED. SPORADIC CRIES, MOANS, ESCALATING GRADUALLY.

TECHS AND GUARDS EYED EACH OTHER. SWIG PACED, BUT NO ONE ATTEMPTED TO STOP THE NOISE.

LOUDER AND LOUDER, FRANTIC POUNDING FROM WITHIN THE CELLS.

THE INMATES KNEW. SOMEHOW, THEY KNEW

HOW COULD PEAKE HAVE GOTTEN OFF THIS FLOOR?

HE COULDN'T. WE'VE CHECKED EVERY DOOR.

AND YET. WHAT ABOUT THE ELEVATOR HATTERSON BROUGHT US UP ON?

PEAKE AND HEIDI WERE WALKING NEAR THERE YESTERDAY. MAYBE HE NOTICED IT.

SWIG CALLED THE ELEVATOR WITH HIS KEY. THE CAR RUMBLED TO LIFE SOMEWHERE BELOW.

YOU CAN ONLY SUMMON THE CAR WITH A KEY, AND ONLY STAFF HAS KEYS.

WHEN WAS THE LAST TIME YOU REMASTERED THE LOCKS?

I'D HAVE TO CHECK. WHAT ARE YOU GETTING AT?

NOT A THING. JUST MARVELING AT THE SECURITY AROUND HERE.

IS THAT YOUR **JOB** HERE TONIGHT, DETECTIVE? **INSULTING** ME AND OUR OPERATIONS WHILE—

JUST TRYING TO FIGURE OUT **HOW** PEAKE GOT OUT, AND TO GET HIM BACK, **WITHOUT** ANY MORE BODIES.

THIS PAPER....LOOKS LIKE THE SANDALS THE INMATES WEAR.

I SUPPOSE IT **COULD** BE. I DON'T SEE ANY BLOOD.

WHY **WOULD** YOU? NO BLOOD TRAIL FROM PEAKE'S ROOM, SO HE STEPPED AWAY AS HE CUT.

NOT **BAD** FOR A **CRAZY** MAN.

HARD TO **BELIEVE** HE COULD—

LOCK THE ELEVATOR. I WANT THE CRIME-SCENE PEOPLE TO SEE IT **JUST** THE WAY IT IS. NOW, LET'S TALK TO YOUR STAFF.

SWIG GATHERED THE TECHS WHO'D BEEN ON DUTY: DORSEY, MILLER, AND QUAN.

MILLER HAD *FOUND* THE BODY.

WE WERE IN LOCKDOWN. WE ALWAYS DO THAT DURING STAFF MEETINGS.

THE PATIENTS GET LOCKED IN, AND STAFF GOES TO THE MEETING, ASIDE FROM *ONE* TECH.

AND DOLLARD WAS THE ONE TONIGHT?

RIGHT. I LOOKED FOR HIM *AFTER* THE MEETING... FOUND PEAKE'S DOOR UNLOCKED.

DOLLARD CARRY A KNIFE?

NONE OF THE STAFF IS *ARMED*, DETECTIVE.

WE HAVE STRICT RULES.

SO IF I FRISK THESE MEN RIGHT NOW, I'LL COME UP EMPTY-HANDED?

OF COURSE.

GENTLEMEN?

YEAH...I CARRY SOMETHING. SO WHAT?

WORKING WITH THESE ANIMALS, YOU HAVE TO PROTECT YOURSELF.

HEY, MAN...THAT'S MINE!

YOU'LL GET IT BACK, IF IT'S CLEAN.

LET'S STOP PRETENDING THIS PLACE IS AIRTIGHT AND LOOK FOR PEAKE ACCORDINGLY.

YOU THINK WE'RE A BUNCH OF INCOMPETENT CIVIL SERVANTS, BUT AS A RULE, NOTHING EVER—

WELL, SOME PEOPLE LIVE FOR THE RULES.

ME, I DEAL WITH THE EXCEPTIONS.

WITHOUT ANOTHER WORD TO MILO, SWIG ORDERED HIS TECHS TO RETURN TO THE SEARCH.

TOO **HARD** ON THE WEASEL?

NO HARDER THAN HIS **BOSSES** WILL BE.

BEFORE WE LOSE THESE GUYS, WHAT ABOUT GEORGE ORSON?

WORTH A **SHOT.** HEY, DORSEY.

WHEN'S THE **LAST** TIME YOU SAW GEORGE ORSON?

ORSON? BEEN AWHILE. HE HASN'T WORKED HERE FOR MONTHS.

WHO IS GEORGE ORSON?

ONE OF YOUR FORMER EMPLOYEES. DON'T **REMEMBER** HIM?

WHAT? NO... I CAN'T RECALL—

DIRECTOR SWIG! THEY'RE **CALLING** FOR YOU OUTSIDE, IMMEDIATELY!

THE HOLE IN THE FENCE WAS **MAN-SIZED**, AND HAD BEEN PULLED BACK INTO PLACE. IT HAD TAKEN A CAREFUL EYE TO SPOT IT.

BY THE TIME WE'D MADE THE HALF MILE WALK TO THE PERIMETER, THE SHERIFF'S OFFICE WAS THERE IN **FORCE**. NINE CARS, VANS, AND A CHOPPER SPOTLIGHTING THE SCENE FROM ABOVE.

SWIG TOLERATED THEIR PRESENCE, MAINLY SPENDING HIS TIME MUTTERING INTO HIS WALKIE TALKIE.

CRIMINOLOGISTS DESCENDED ON PEAKE'S ROOM...THE CRIME SCENE, AS WELL AS THE ELEVATOR AND CONNECTING CORRIDORS.

INITIAL FINDINGS CONFIRMED MILO'S SUSPICIONS: DOLLARD'S CAROTID HAD BEEN NICKED, AND RATHER **EXPERTLY**. HE'D BLED OUT WHERE HE FELL. NO SPATTER...MOST OF THE BLOOD POOLED UNDER THE BODY.

AND, THE PAPER IN THE ELEVATOR APPEARED TO BE PART OF AN INMATE'S SLIPPER.

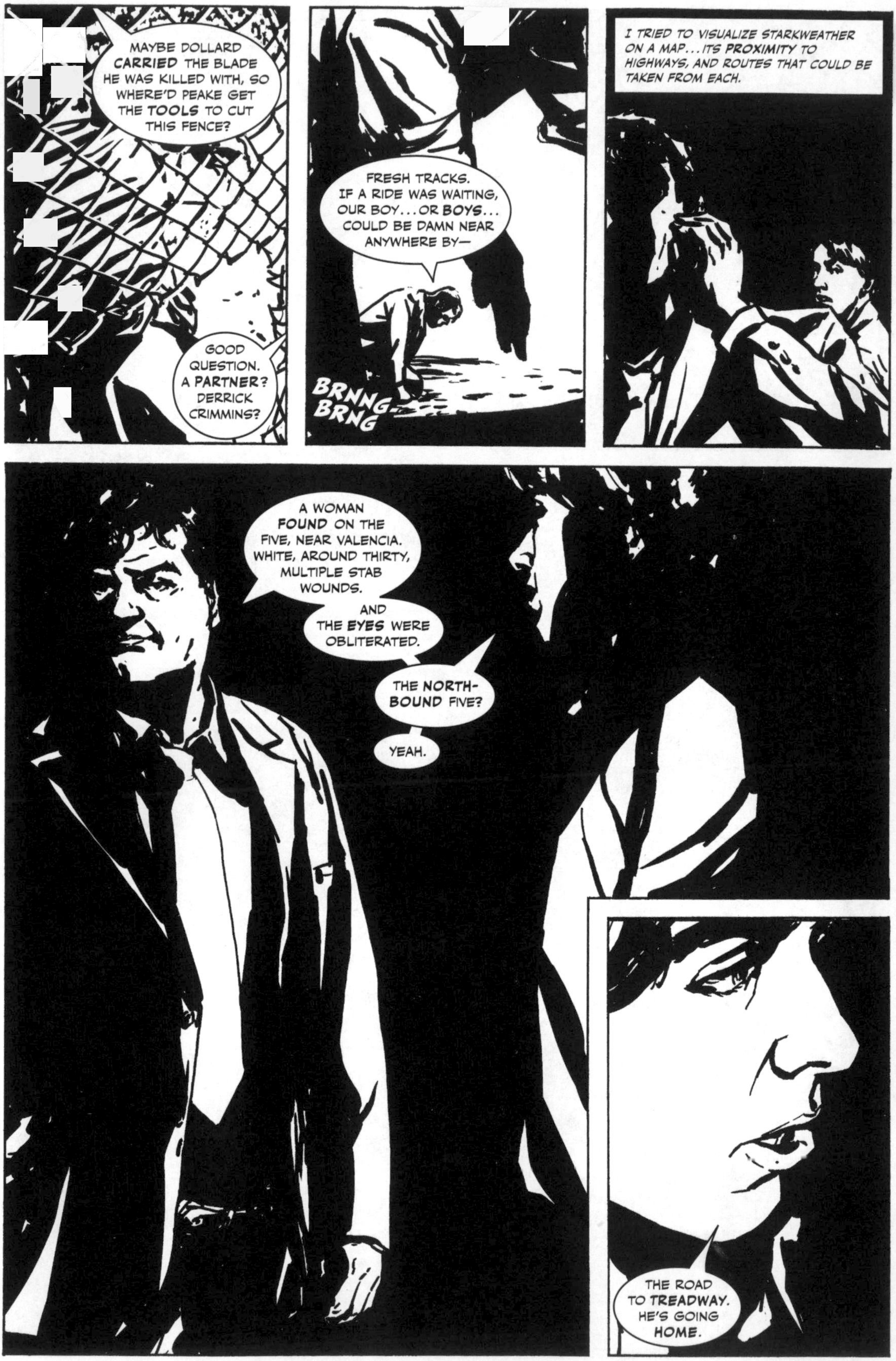
MAYBE DOLLARD CARRIED THE BLADE HE WAS KILLED WITH, SO WHERE'D PEAKE GET THE TOOLS TO CUT THIS FENCE?
GOOD QUESTION. A PARTNER? DERRICK CRIMMINS?
FRESH TRACKS. IF A RIDE WAS WAITING, OUR BOY...OR BOYS... COULD BE DAMN NEAR ANYWHERE BY—
BRNNG BRNNG
I TRIED TO VISUALIZE STARKWEATHER ON A MAP...ITS PROXIMITY TO HIGHWAYS, AND ROUTES THAT COULD BE TAKEN FROM EACH.
A WOMAN FOUND ON THE FIVE, NEAR VALENCIA. WHITE, AROUND THIRTY, MULTIPLE STAB WOUNDS.
AND THE EYES WERE OBLITERATED.
THE NORTH-BOUND FIVE?
YEAH.
THE ROAD TO TREADWAY. HE'S GOING HOME.

CRIMMINS AT STARKWEATHER. BACK WITH PEAKE...JUST LIKE THE GOOD OLD DAYS.

HE WORKED THERE **PLENTY** LONG ENOUGH TO COPY THE KEYS TO EVERY DOOR.

HE'D DOMINATED PEAKE **BEFORE**...KNOWS HE'S PASSIVE. HE SLIPS HIM THE **KNIFE**. CUES HIM THAT THE TIME IS RIGHT.

DOLLARD WAS A SLACKER...OR **WORSE**. MAYBE HE WAS **PART** OF THE DRUG SCAM, HELPING DERRICK SNEAK STUFF OUT.

WITH US **SNIFFING** AROUND DERRICK DECIDES DOLLARD KNOWS TOO MUCH. CRIMMINS HAS A HISTORY OF TYING UP LOOSE ENDS.

HOW DOES **CLAIRE** FIT IN?

SHE DIS-**COVERED** THE DRUG SCHEME, OR WAS **PART** OF IT, TOO.

OR, MAYBE SHE DID THE **ONE** THING DERRICK COULDN'T ALLOW...**LISTENED** TO PEAKE.

MAYBE SHE **LEARNED** HE HADN'T ACTED ALONE WITH THE ARDULLOS.

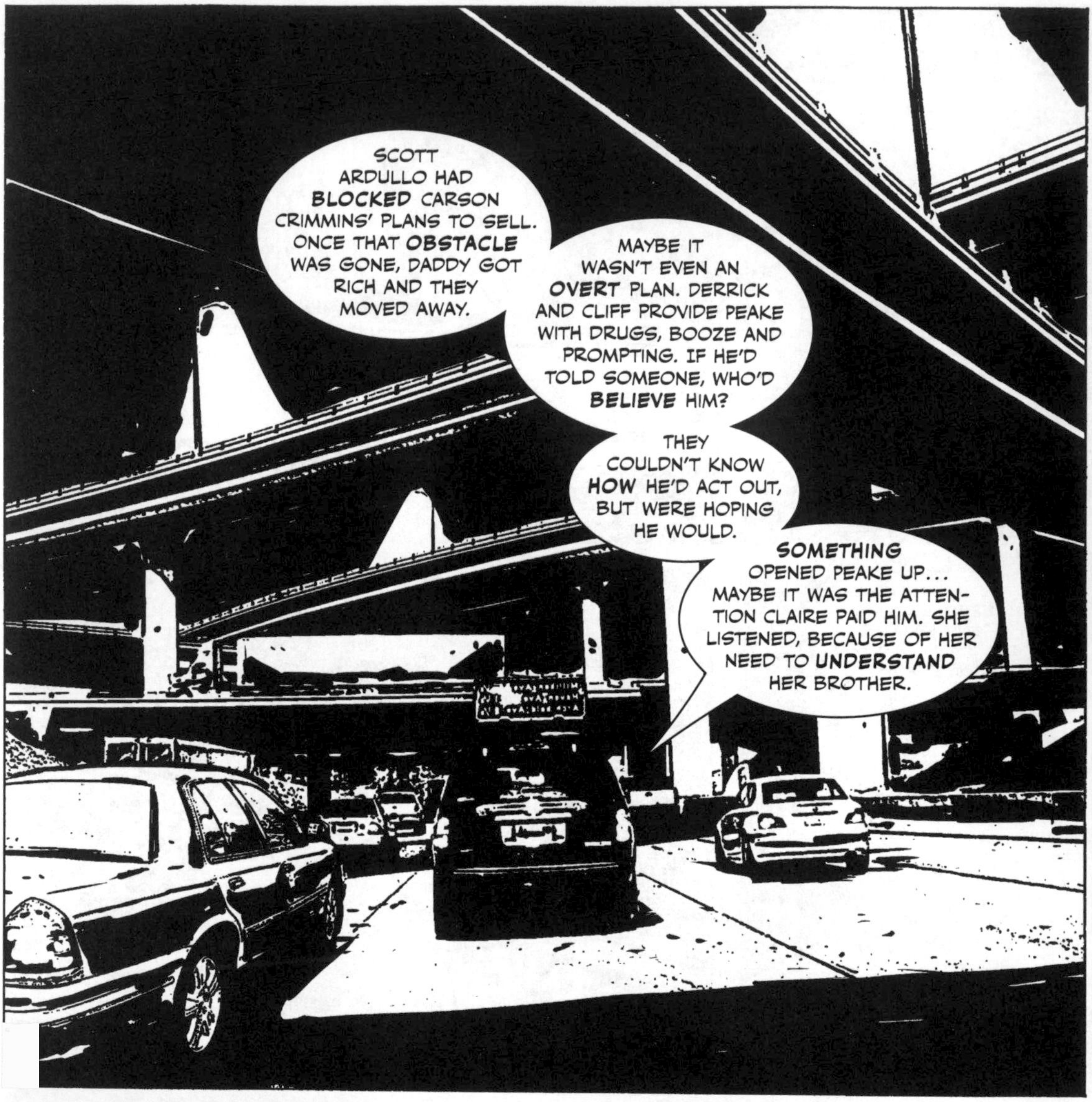
SCOTT ARDULLO HAD BLOCKED CARSON CRIMMINS' PLANS TO SELL. ONCE THAT OBSTACLE WAS GONE, DADDY GOT RICH AND THEY MOVED AWAY.
MAYBE IT WASN'T EVEN AN OVERT PLAN. DERRICK AND CLIFF PROVIDE PEAKE WITH DRUGS, BOOZE AND PROMPTING. IF HE'D TOLD SOMEONE, WHO'D BELIEVE HIM?
THEY COULDN'T KNOW HOW HE'D ACT OUT, BUT WERE HOPING HE WOULD.
SOMETHING OPENED PEAKE UP... MAYBE IT WAS THE ATTENTION CLAIRE PAID HIM. SHE LISTENED, BECAUSE OF HER NEED TO UNDERSTAND HER BROTHER.

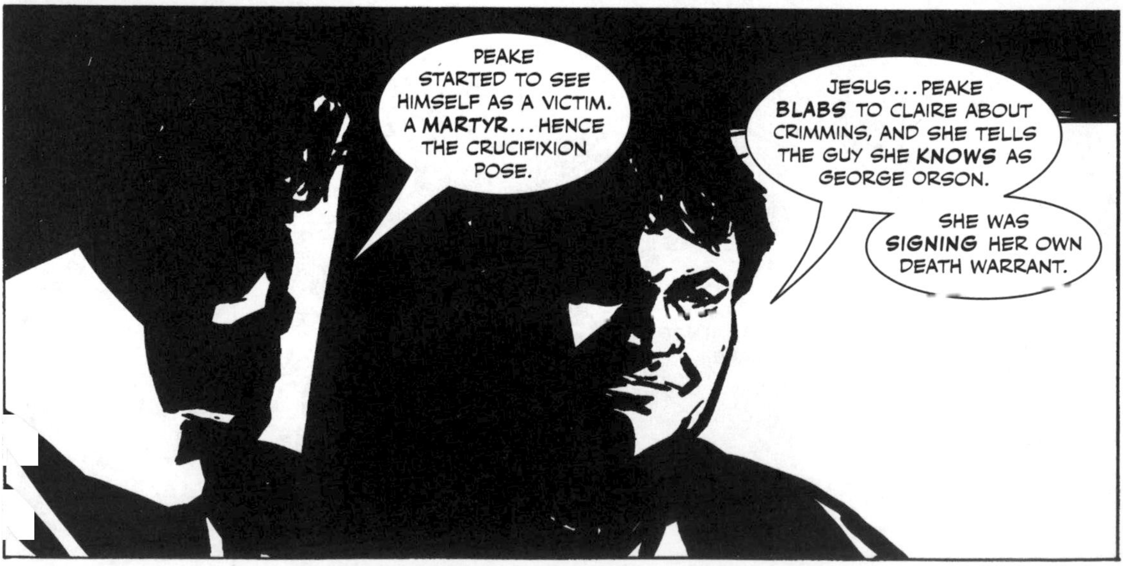
PEAKE STARTED TO SEE HIMSELF AS A VICTIM. A MARTYR... HENCE THE CRUCIFIXION POSE.
JESUS... PEAKE BLABS TO CLAIRE ABOUT CRIMMINS, AND SHE TELLS THE GUY SHE KNOWS AS GEORGE ORSON.
SHE WAS SIGNING HER OWN DEATH WARRANT.

SO, IS **PEAKE** JUST ANOTHER LOOSE END? HOW DOES THAT **WORK** IF HE'S THE ONE WHO SLICED THE WOMAN ON THE I-FIVE?

I'M NOT SURE, BUT IN THIS CASE **MONSTER** AND **VICTIM** AREN'T MUTUALLY EXCLUSIVE.

BY THE WAY, THAT FENCE WASN'T CUT **TONIGHT**...OXIDATION AROUND THE EDGES.

PEAKE'S ESCAPE WAS REHEARSED, LIKE ANY PRODUCTION. IS **THAT** WHAT TREADWAY IS...MORE **THEATER**?

JUST PART OF DERRICK'S **SCRIPT**.

SO WHY LEAVE THE WOMAN ON THE FREEWAY? IT DIRECTS **ATTENTION** TO HIS PLAN.

YEAH. HELL, MILO...MAYBE I'M **TOTALLY** OFF-BASE.

MAYBE THE ESCAPE WAS A **ONE-MAN** OPERATION. MAYBE PEAKE REALLY IS A CALCULATING MONSTER.

DESTROYING. REDUCING EYES TO PULP, **STARTING** WITH THE ARDULLOS...

I KNEW WHO **SHE** WAS WITHIN SECONDS.

THE EYES WERE TWO OVERSIZED RASPBERRIES. THE FACE LOST TO A CRIMSON GRID OF SLASHES.

THE NECK WAS UNTOUCHED, THOUGH, AND IT WAS THERE I SAW THE **FRECKLES.**

MILO SPOKE TO THE **PATROLMAN** ON THE SCENE...A YOUNG, ENORMOUS MAN NAMED WHITWORTH...

...AS I CONTINUED TO STARE AT WHAT WAS **LEFT** OF THE YOUNG WOMAN WE'D MET AS **HEIDI OTT.**

WHITWORTH SAID SHE'D BEEN SHOT POINT BLANK IN THE BACK OF THE HEAD.

FIRST...**BEFORE** THE BUTCHERY.

I PICTURED THE THREE OF THEM: CRIMMINS, PEAKE AND HEIDI, IN A CAR THAT PULLED OVER ABRUPTLY.

WAS SHE A PASSENGER OR A **HOSTAGE** AT THAT POINT?

HAD SHE ASKED DERRICK WHAT WAS UP?

IN THOSE MOMENTS BEFORE THE MUZZLE FLASH, HAD SHE **SUSPECTED**?

WHAT WAS THE **LAST** THING SHE'D HEARD? A TRUCK WHIZZING BY? THE WIND?

THE **RACING** OF HER PULSE?

CRIMMINS GIVES A **SIGNAL**...PEAKE STEPS FORWARD, BLADE IN HAND.

CAMERA. ACTION. CUT.

THEY GOT A HIT FROM PRINTS TAKEN FROM THE BODY. HER **REAL** NAME WAS HEDY LYNN HAUPT.

HAS A PREVIOUS BUST FOR POSSESSION. COKE.

AND, **THANKS** TO PATROLMAN WHITWORTH, WE HAVE A LAST KNOWN **ADDRESS.**

HEIDI OTT—HEDY HAUPT—LIVED IN WEST HOLLYWOOD, NOT FAR FROM PLUMMER PARK, WHERE SHE'D FIRST ASKED US TO MEET.

"MY ROOMMATE'S SLEEPING," SHE'D SAID, "OR I WOULD'VE HAD YOU COME TO MY PLACE."

MILO HAD **SHOULDERED** THE BACK DOOR AND CLEARED THE HOUSE BEFORE WE BEGAN OUR SEARCH.

THE GARAGE HELD THE MOVIE EQUIPMENT, STACKED ALMOST TO THE CEILING, ALONG WITH BOXES OF VIDEO CASSETTE TAPES. IT WOULD TAKE A POLICE TEAM **DAYS** TO GO THROUGH IT ALL.

SOMETHING IN THE LIVING ROOM CAUGHT MY EYE.

GEARS TURNED AS I CONNECTED THE DOTS, FEELING SILLY FOR NOT SEEING IT SOONER.

PHENOBARBITAL, CHLORPROMAZINE, CLOZAPINE...YOU **NAME** IT. UNCUT PHARMACEUTI-CALS, **STRAIGHT** FROM STARKWEATHER.

SHE WAS IN ON IT.

OH, YEAH.

YOU NOTICE THE **DOG BOWL** IN THE LIVING ROOM?

NO. WHY?

JUST SOME-THING I **SHOULD** HAVE SEEN A LONG TIME AGO...

"THERE WAS A MISSING DOG POSTER OUTSIDE CRIMMING' HOUSE. THE DOG LOOKED FAMILIAR, BUT I COULDN'T PLACE IT."

HAVE YOU SEEN **BUDDY**

$100 REWARD

"WHEN I SAW THE BOWL HERE IT **CLICKED**. THERE WAS A DOG THERE IN THE PARK, WHEN WE MET HEIDI."

"A DOG BEING WALKED BY A TALL, SKINNY MAN IN BLACK."

"HE PASSED **RIGHT** BY US. HEIDI SEEMED NERVOUS ABOUT HIM."

SHIT. DERRICK WAS THE **ROOMMATE**... THE ONE SHE SAID WAS SLEEPING. THEIR LITTLE JOKE.

THEY PLAYED US **RIGHT** FROM THE BEGINNING.

PEAKE'S "PROPHECY." ANOTHER SCAM.

HAS TO BE. THE ONLY **EVIDENCE** WE HAD WAS HEIDI'S ACCOUNT.

THE DAMN **TAPE**, TOO...A BUNCH OF UNRECOGNIZABLE MUMBLES.

THE **VOICE** OF GEORGE WELLES ORSON. **SONOFA-BITCH!**

HE **MURDERED** CLAIRE, THEN SET **PEAKE** UP AS A PHONY ORACLE TO SPICE UP HIS STORY LINE. SCREWING THE LAW AGAIN, LIKE HE'D DONE IN FLORIDA. **AND** NEVADA. **AND** TREADWAY.

HEIDI JOINED THE STAFF AT STARKWEATHER RIGHT **AFTER** ORSON LEFT. SHE WAS HIS INSIDE WOMAN, WITH **DUAL** ASSIGNMENTS: KEEPING THE DRUGS FLOWING AND KEEPING DIBS ON PEAKE.

SHE WAS SO **CALM** WITH US. AN **ACTRESS**...COOL UNDER PRESSURE. THE MOMENT WE WERE GONE SHE WAS ON THE PHONE TO CRIMMINS.

EVENTUALLY HE **KNEW** WE WERE GETTING TOO CLOSE, SO A **NEW** PLAN, USING HEIDI... GET RID OF DOLLARD AND BREAK PEAKE LOOSE.

MAKES ME WONDER WHO **ACTUALLY** KILLED DOLLARD...HEIDI OR PEAKE?

MILO WANTED TO **SEARCH** THE PLACE BEFORE WE REJOINED THE PURSUIT OF CRIMMINS AND PEAKE. WE WENT THROUGH THE BEDROOM AND KITCHEN, WORKING QUICKLY.

THE LIVING ROOM HELD THE MOST INTERESTING DISCOVERIES. I FOUND A BOX FULL OF DISGUISES: WIGS, TOUPEES, FAKE NOSES MADE OF LATEX.

MILO FOUND SOME WHITE POWDER IN A GLASSINE ENVELOPE. COCAINE, ALONG WITH A BOX OF POPPERS.

I FOUND A LOOSE-LEAF NOTEBOOK UNDER THE SOFA.

MILO...

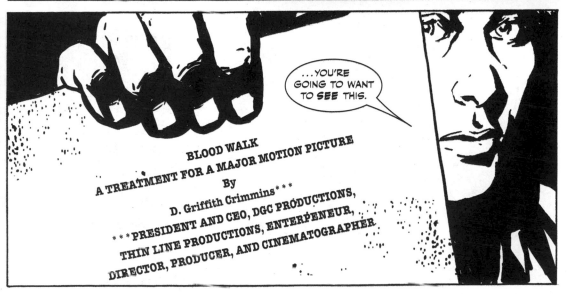

...YOU'RE GOING TO WANT TO **SEE** THIS.

BLOOD WALK
A TREATMENT FOR A MAJOR MOTION PICTURE
By
D. Griffith Crimmins***
***PRESIDENT AND CEO, DGC PRODUCTIONS,
THIN LINE PRODUCTIONS, ENTERPENEUR,
DIRECTOR, PRODUCER, AND CINEMATOGRAPHER

PAGE AFTER PAGE, SOILED, SMUDGED AND MOSTLY WRITTEN IN BALLPOINT.

ONE EARLY PAGE LISTED ALTERNATE TITLES, HALF OF WHICH WERE MISSPELLED: "THE MONSTER RETURNS," "DAREDEVIL AVENGER: JUSTISE FOR ALL," AND "THE THIN LINE...WHO'S TO SAY WHOS CRAZY AND WHOS NOT."

"DARE-DEVIL AVENGER." HE SEES *HIMSELF* AS THE RISK-TAKER...THE HERO.

MAYBE SAVING THE WORLD FROM PEAKE?

HE LIKED "THIN LINE" SO MUCH HE USED IT AS THE NAME OF HIS COMPANY.

WHO'S TO SAY WHO'S NUTS? I SAY, ASSHOLE...AND YOU ARE.

YOU *HEAR* THAT?

THE LIGHT IN THE ROOM CHANGED...PASSING HEADLIGHTS. A CAR SETTLED INTO AN IDLE IN THE DRIVEWAY.

THE ENGINE DIED. A DOOR OPENED AND CLOSED. FOOTSTEPS SCRAPED THE DRIVEWAY.

DIMINISHING FOOTSTEPS.

SHIT. STAY PUT.

I DIDN'T.

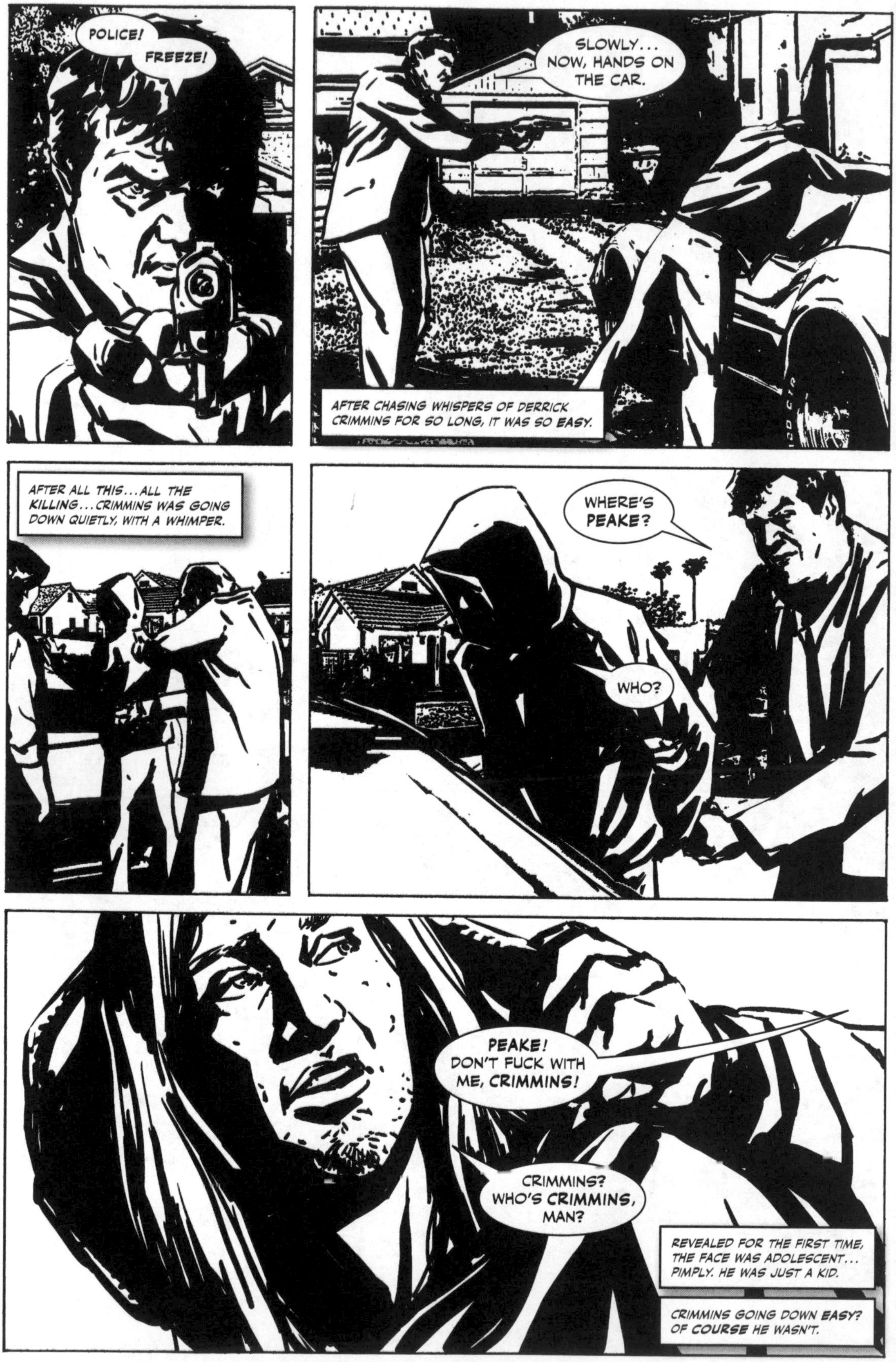
POLICE!
FREEZE!
SLOWLY... NOW, HANDS ON THE CAR.
AFTER CHASING WHISPERS OF DERRICK CRIMMINS FOR SO LONG, IT WAS SO EASY.
AFTER ALL THIS... ALL THE KILLING... CRIMMINS WAS GOING DOWN QUIETLY, WITH A WHIMPER.
WHERE'S PEAKE?
WHO?
PEAKE! DON'T FUCK WITH ME, CRIMMINS!
CRIMMINS? WHO'S CRIMMINS, MAN?
REVEALED FOR THE FIRST TIME, THE FACE WAS ADOLESCENT... PIMPLY. HE WAS JUST A KID.
CRIMMINS GOING DOWN EASY? OF COURSE HE WASN'T.

ALL RIGHT, **SOAMES**...RUN THIS **BULLSHIT** STORY BY ME ONE MORE TIME.

LEMME LOOGE, MAN. I DIN'T DO **NOTHIN'.**

HIS NAME WAS CHRISTOPHER PAUL SOAMES, AND HE HAD I.D. TO PROVE IT...A PHONY CALIFORNIA DRIVER'S LICENSE AND A THREE-YEAR-OLD STUDENT CARD FROM BELLFLOWER HIGH.

RIGHT. SOME DUDE JUST **HANDED** YOU THE KEYS TO THE 'VETTE.

ASKS YOU TO DRIVE IT **HOME** FOR HIM, AND GIVES YOU TWENTY BUCKS AS A THANKS.

THAT'S **RIGHT!**

WHAT IF I TOLD YOU, CHRIS, THAT I **BELIEVE** YOU?

WHAT IF I TOLD YOU I **KNOW** WHAT THIS DUDE LOOKED LIKE? TALL, SKINNY, BIG NOSE, DRESSES ALL IN **BLACK.** PROBABLY A WIG.

YOU'RE **LUCKY** TO BE ALIVE, CHRIS. THIS GUY LIKES TO KILL PEOPLE. LIKES TO MAKE IT HURT.

YOU'RE **BULLSHITTING,** MAN. YOU **HAVE** TO BE!

OH, **JESUS**...I LET HIM TAKE **SUZY!**

I WATCHED SOAMES WHILE MILO CALLED IN FOR DETAILS ON A SUSANNA GALVEZ.

IT WAS SINKING IN FOR THE KID NOW... ALL OF IT, INCLUDING HANDING HIS GIRLFRIEND OVER TO A KILLER.

MISSING-PERSONS REPORT FILED BY SUSANNA'S PARENTS LAST YEAR. THEY SUSPECT SHE'S WITH HER BOYFRIEND.

MALE, CAUCASIAN, BLOND AND BLUE...GOES BY THE NAME OF CHRIS.

SHE'S ONLY FOURTEEN!

IF SHE'S GOING TO SEE FIFTEEN, YOU'D BETTER TELL IT ALL, YOU LITTLE SHIT. NOW!

OKAY, MAN... OKAY. I'VE SEEN THE DUDE BEFORE. HE CRUISES HOLLYWOOD. NEVER IN THE 'VETTE BEFORE. USUALLY A BLACK JEEP.

SUZY AND ME CALLED HIM MARILYN, 'CAUSE HE'S TALL AND WEIRD-LOOKIN'... LIKE MARILYN MANSON. HIM AND HIS GIRLFRIEND...THEY GOT PILLS, MAN. PRESCRIPTION SHIT.

SO TONIGHT HE ROLLS UP IN THE 'VETTE. SAYS HE KNOWS HE CAN TRUST ME, AND HE NEEDS A FAVOR. GIVES ME TWENTY TO DROP THE CAR HERE AND TAKE THE BUS BACK.

SAYS HE'LL GIVE ME ANOTHER FIFTY TOMORROW MORNING. SAYS HE'LL GIVE ME SUZY BACK THEN, TOO.

SAID HE'S MAKING A MOVIE AND SUZY'S PRETTY...HE COULD USE HER!

DEPUTIES ARRIVED WITHIN TEN MINUTES. MILO HANDED SOAMES OVER AND WE HEADED OUT AGAIN.

BY NOW MILO KNEW *BETTER* THAN TO ASK ME IF I WAS COMING WITH HIM.

TWO CARS. TWO DRIVERS.

CRIMMINS *KNEW* HEIDI WOULDN'T BE AROUND LONG. HE NEEDED SOMEONE TO PARK THE 'VETTE.

HE GIVES THE JOB TO AN *IDIOT* LIKE SOAMES BECAUSE HE DOESN'T REALLY *CARE* IF IT GETS *DONE*.

YEAH... SO WHAT DOES THAT *MEAN* FOR SUSANNA GALVEZ?

TONIGHT MARKS THE *BEGINNING* OF A NEW ERA FOR DERRICK.

THE GUYS WHO KILLED HEIDI ARE ABOUT TO DO THE **SAME** TO SUSANNA... IN OR NEAR TREADWAY.

WHITWORTH WAS **WAITING** FOR US BACK WHERE HEIDI HAD BEEN KILLED. THE BODY HAD BEEN REMOVED, AND CRIME TECHS SCOURED THE AREA.

MILO FILLED THE PATROLMAN IN.

THEY MIGHT STORM INTO A HOUSE, OR HEAD TOWARD THE MOUNTAINS.

NOT GONNA BE AN EVEREST THING...NOT WITH PEAKE AND WHATEVER MOVIE EQUIPMENT CRIMMINS HAS.

ALL RIGHT. I'LL RIDE OUT WITH YOU ON MY BIKE, AND I'LL CALL IN **SUPPORT.**

WHAT ABOUT **CHOPPERS?** WOULD NOISE AND LIGHTS STOP HIM OR EGG HIM ON?

DEPENDS ON THE SCRIPT.

IF **CORNERED,** HE MIGHT FOLD, OR HE MIGHT GO FOR THE BIG ENDING.

PUT THE CHOPPERS ON **STANDBY.** WE'LL GO IN QUIET AND PLAY IT BY EAR.

YOU CAN FOL-LOW US...ALEX IS THE ONLY ONE WHO'S ACTUALLY BEEN TO THE PLACE.

SOME MAIL STACKED UP. I'D SAY THEY'VE BEEN GONE FOR A DAY OR TWO.

WHEN WE GOT TO TREADWAY I MENTIONED JACOB HAAS, THE MAN WHO'D ARRESTED PEAKE, AS A POTENTIAL REVENGE TARGET.

ONE OF THEIR CARS IS GONE. THEY'RE PROBABLY AWAY...VISITING RELATIVES.

DETECTIVE, YOU SEE ANY CAUSE FOR BREAKING IN?

NO. ANY IDEAS, ALEX?

WHO KNOWS IF MY HUNCHES ARE WORTH A DAMN. MAYBE THEY DIDN'T COME TO TREADWAY AT ALL.

BUT, IF THEY DID...

...THE MOUNTAINS WOULD BE A HELL OF A SETTING FOR A FINAL SCENE.

TIRE TRACKS. JEB THE TRACKER I AIN'T, BUT THEY LOOK NEW TO ME.

THE ONLY CLEAR PATH FROM THE COMMUNITY TOWARD THE DESERT WAS A SHORT ACCESS ROAD.

I'LL HAVE SUPPORT HERE IN TWENTY MINUTES, MAYBE. SAME WITH THE CHOPPER.

IF DERRICK'S OUT THERE, SO IS SUSANNA GALVEZ. HE COULD KILL HER ANY MINUTE.

AGREED, BUT A VEHICLE OUT THERE, EVEN WITH-OUT LIGHTS, WOULD BE SPOTTED A MILE AWAY. ALEX, YOUR INSTINCTS GOT US THIS FAR. FEEL LIKE A STROLL?

HE DIDN'T REALLY HAVE TO ASK.

I'LL FINISH SEARCHING THE NEIGHBOR-HOOD. STAY IN TOUCH.

IF WE FIND THE SON-OFABITCH, YOU'LL BE THE FIRST TO KNOW.

AND, ALEX, HOLD UP A MINUTE...

"...ROBIN WOULD NEVER **FORGIVE** ME IF I LET YOU GET KILLED WITHOUT SOME **PROTECTION**."

IT LOOKED TO BE ABOUT TWO MILES FROM THE HOMES OF TREADWAY TO THE BASE OF THE TEHACHAPIS. AFTER TWENTY MINUTES WE HAD TO BE **HALFWAY** THERE, BUT THE MOUNTAINS LOOKED NO CLOSER.

I TRIED NOT TO THINK ABOUT SUSANNA GALVEZ...ABOUT **WHATEVER** CRIMMINS AND PEAKE HAD PLANNED FOR HER. I THOUGHT AGAIN ABOUT HEIDI IN THOSE FINAL MOMENTS. WAS SUSANNA AHEAD OF US **SOMEWHERE**, A GUN PRESSED TO THE BACK OF HER HEAD? WAS SHE **ALREADY** DEAD?

WAS PEAKE ATTACKING **HER** EYES WITH A BLADE, REDUCING THEM TO PULP?

OR WERE THEY ALL MILES **AWAY**? DERRICK PLAYING OUT HIS FINAL ACT WITHOUT RISK OR INTRUSION, BECAUSE I'D FOLLOWED THE **WRONG HUNCH**?

WHETHER HE'S OUT HERE OR **NOT**, THIS IS THE BEST LEAD WE'VE GOT.

BESIDES, BASED ON HOW THIS THING HAS PLAYED OUT **SO** FAR...

MILO MUST HAVE **SENSED** MY DOUBTS.

...IT'D BE JUST **LIKE** CRIMMINS TO MAKE ME **HIKE** THROUGH THIS FUCKING DESERT.

NEITHER OF US **LAUGHED**.

I **STUMBLED** ALONG, KEEPING MY EYES GLUED TO THE MOUNTAINS, SEEING **NOTHING**...

...UNTIL A PINPOINT OF LIGHT DANCED AGAINST SHEER STONE...

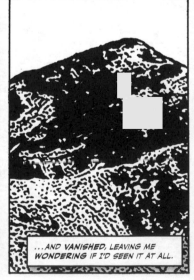

...AND **VANISHED**, LEAVING ME WONDERING IF I'D SEEN IT AT ALL.

THE LIGHT **REAPPEARED**, BOUNCING AGAINST THE MOUNTAIN. MILO SAW IT, TOO.

A CAMERA LIGHT. MAYBE SHE'S STILL **ALIVE**.

SHIT... NO **SIGNAL**.

WHITWORTH CALLING IN THE CHOPPER IS **OUT**, AT LEAST FOR NOW.

ALL RIGHT, WE GO IN **ALONE**.

SLOW AND QUIET...

...EVEN IT IT **FEELS** LIKE IT'LL TAKE **FOREVER**.

THE LIGHT BECAME MORE CONSTANT AND BRIGHTER AS WE CLIMBED, AND WAS **JOINED** BY SOUNDS.

THE WHIRRING AND CLICKING OF A STILL CAMERA.

NO TELLING IF THIS WILL PLAY OUT UP **CLOSE** OR AT A DISTANCE...

...BUT I THINK WE SHOULD **TRADE** WEAPONS.

JUST **FOLLOW** MY LEAD, AND BE **READY** WITH THAT THING.

SHARP-EDGED BOULDERS ROSE AHEAD, FORMING A CIRCLE WE WERE **SHIELDED** FROM. A NATURAL STUDIO.

NEW SOUNDS...LOW, UNINTELLIGIBLE SPEECH. **LAUGHTER.**

WE MADE OUR WAY **AROUND A** BOULDER AND INTO THE EDGE OF THE CLEARING.

THE TABLEAU DERRICK CRIMMINS HAD **CREATED** CAME INTO VIEW.

PLENTY OF LIGHT *NOW*. AN EXTENSION CORD CONNECTED A SPOTLIGHT TO A BATTERY PACK. THE BULB WAS AIMED DOWNWARD, WELL SHORT OF THE FIFTEEN-FOOT WALLS THAT SURROUNDED THE CLEARING.

SUSANNA GALVEZ WAS *ALIVE*, OR APPEARED TO BE. HER EYES STARED AT NOTHING, IMMOBILE AND MAD WITH TERROR.

I HAD ONLY MET MARVELLE HAAS IN *PASSING*, BUT I RECOGNIZED HER. JACOB MUST HAVE GONE AWAY BY *HIMSELF*, LEAVING HER HOME ALONE.

HAD HE MOVED INTO *REVERIE*?

THE CAMERAMAN *PRODDED* PEAKE, CURSING...ENCOURAGING.

LONG WHITE FINGERS SNAKED THEIR WAY AROUND THE GUN.

PEAKE HELD THE GUN TO MARVELLE'S HEAD, BUT SHOWED NO SIGN HE WAS ENJOYING THE TORMENT.

ADJUSTING THE GUN IN PEAKE'S HAND, AND NOW I *NOTICED* SOMETHING.

THE WEAPON WAS *HELD* IN THE SPINDLY FINGERS BY TRANSPARENT TAPE.

THE *ARM* WAS HELD IN PLACE, AS WELL.

PEAKE WAS BEING *FORCED* INTO THIS POSE.

FISHING LINE, ALL BUT INVISIBLE, TIED AROUND THE *TRIGGER* OF THE GUN. SPECIAL EFFECTS.

WITHIN THE CAMERAMAN'S *REACH*. ONE SHARP TUG WOULD SEND A BULLET INTO MARVELLE'S BRAIN.

PEAKE'S HEAD ROLLED AS A SEIZURE RAN THROUGH HIS BODY. HIS FINGERS MOVED JUST ENOUGH TO MOVE THE FISHING LINE.

THE CAMERAMAN *LIKED* THAT.

MILO STEPPED AROUND ME *SILENTLY*, THE RIFLE AIMED AND READY...BUT HE COULDN'T FIRE.

IF THE CAMERAMAN *DROPPED* HE COULD FALL ON THE FISHING LINE, *PULLING* THE TRIGGER.

GO FOR IT, YOU *FUCKING* MEAT PUPPET! *KILL* THE BITCH.

SOME FUCKING *MONSTER* YOU ARE.

WHAPP

THE CAMERAMAN *LAUGHED* AS HE NOTICED THE FISHING LINE WAS TAUT.

I WATCHED PEAKE'S HAND. HIS FINGER PULLED *AWAY* FROM THE TRIGGER, DESPITE THE LINE.

HE WAS *RESISTING*.

MILO INCHED **CLOSER**. THE RIFLE WAS TRAINED ON THE BACK OF THE CAMERAMAN'S HEAD...THE MEDULLA OBLONGATA. A **SNIPER'S** TARGET.

IN THE **FLESH**, DERRICK CRIMMINS HAD BECOME A TWISTED, **MONSTROUS** VERSION OF HIS FATHER.

ALL RIGHT, ARDIS...I'VE GOT **ENOUGH** COVERAGE. ONE WAY OR **ANOTHER**...LET'S DO THE BITCH.

OPEN YOUR **EYES**, MRS. HAAS. I WANT TO SEE YOUR EXPRESSION WHEN IT HAPPENS.

CRIMMINS MOVED CLOSER TO MARVELLE, AND **AWAY** FROM THE FISHING LINE.

IT GAVE MILO THE **OPENING** HE'D BEEN WAITING FOR.

DON'T MOVE! DROP YOUR HANDS... NOW!!!

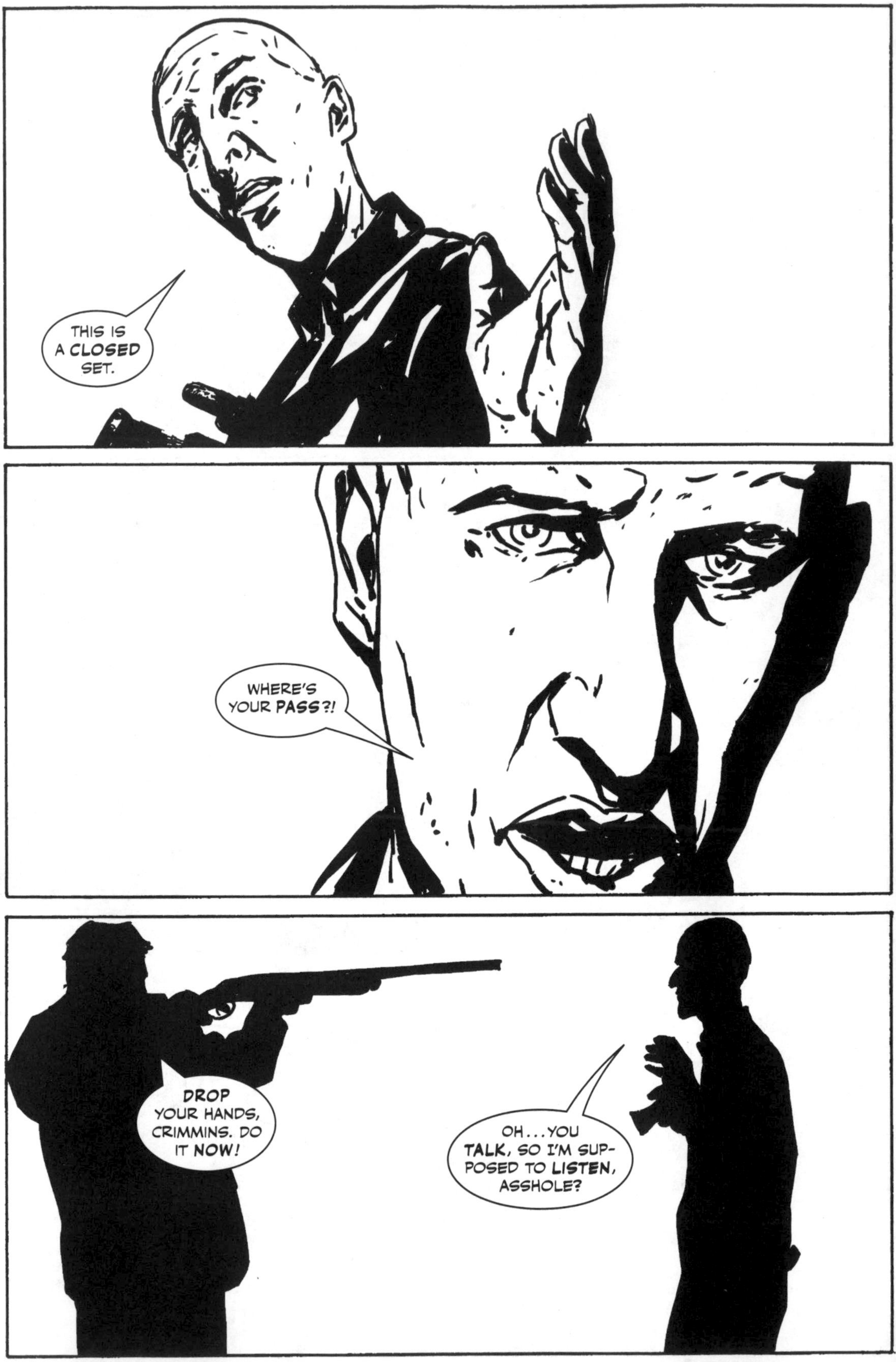
THIS IS A CLOSED SET.
WHERE'S YOUR PASS?!
DROP YOUR HANDS, CRIMMINS. DO IT NOW!
OH...YOU TALK, SO I'M SUP-POSED TO LISTEN, ASSHOLE?

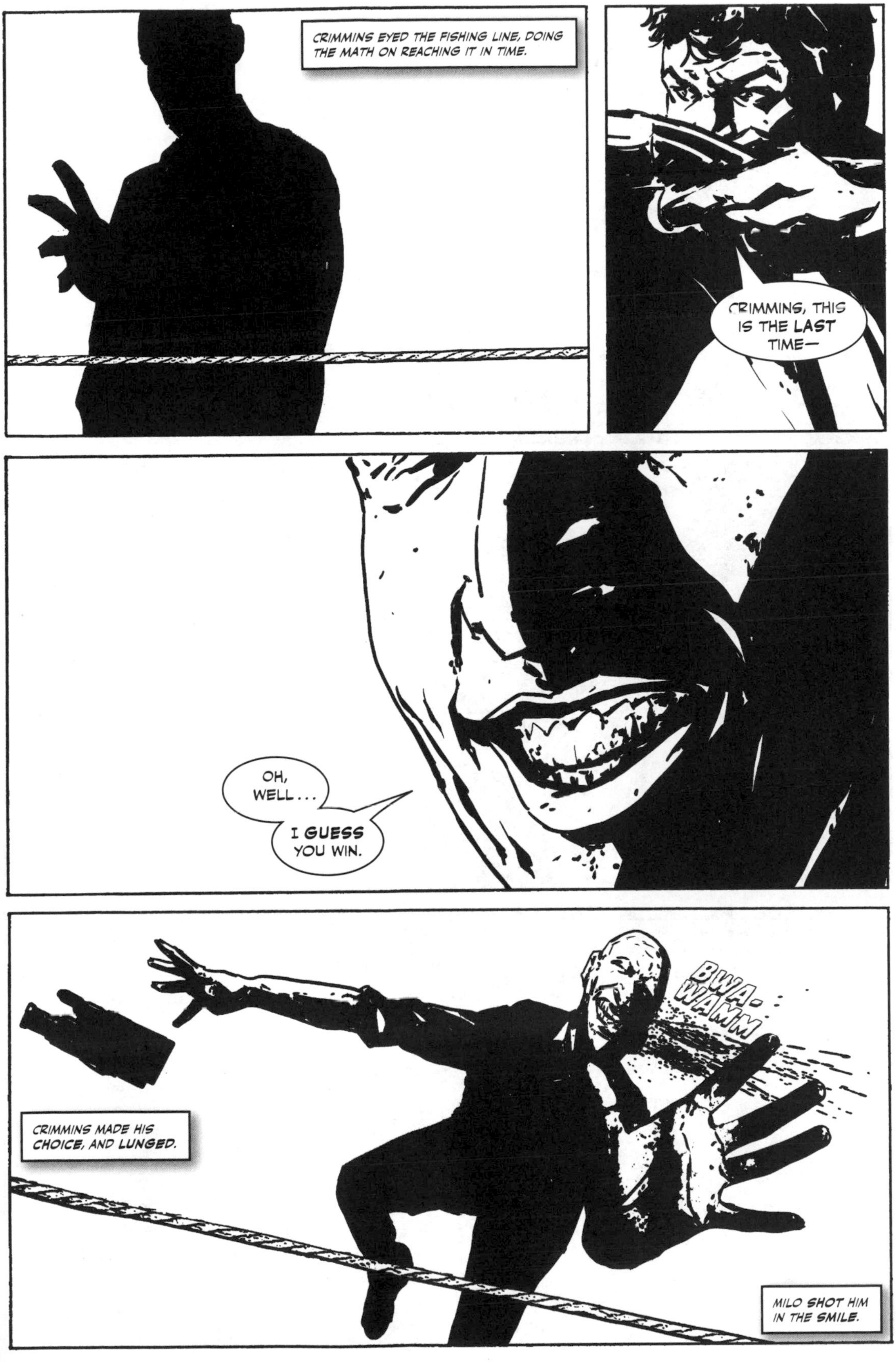
CRIMMINS EYED THE FISHING LINE, DOING THE MATH ON REACHING IT IN TIME.
CRIMMINS, THIS IS THE LAST TIME—
OH, WELL...
I GUESS YOU WIN.
CRIMMINS MADE HIS CHOICE, AND LUNGED.
BWA-WAMM
MILO SHOT HIM IN THE SMILE.

THE PARAPHERNALIA ASSOCIATED WITH DERRICK CRIMMINS'
KILLING SPREE HAD BEEN RECOVERED AT **VARIOUS** SITES: THE
STOLEN FOUR-WHEELER, "HEIDI'S" HOUSE, AND THE MOUNTAIN.

STOLEN PLATES AND REGISTRATIONS, CAMCORDERS,
BARBITURATES, METHAMPHETAMINE, MOTION PICTURE
GEAR...AND **VIDEO** TAPES.

SIXTEEN FILMED DEATH SCENES IN ALL. SOME WERE STILL BEING
I.D.ED, BUT THERE WAS RICHARD DADA, TALKING EXCITEDLY ABOUT
HIS CAREER BEFORE HIS THROAT WAS SLASHED.

STARKWEATHER
STATE HOSPITAL
FOR THE
CRIMINALLY INSANE

CLAIRE ARGENT, CHATTING PSYCHOLOGY
BEFORE BEING SMOTHERED UNDER A PILLOW.

HEDY/HEIDI VAMPING NEAR THE OVERPASS,
BEFORE HER HEAD **DISAPPEARED** IN A FLASH.

ON A SCRIPT PAGE FOUND ON HIS BODY, CRIMMINS
HAD BROKEN DOWN EACH VICTIM BY TYPE.

RICHARD, THE "FAG ACTOR." CLAIRE, THE "OLD-MAID
PROFESSOR." HEIDI, THE "CRACK WHORE."

SUSANNA GALVEZ...SUZY, WAS TO BE THE
"GREASER FARM-CHICK." MARVELLE HAAS,
THE "SHERIFF'S HOT-BLOODED WIFE."

I'D BEEN SEEING SUZY GALVEZ, TRYING TO **HELP** HER BREAK THROUGH POST-TRAUMA SYMPTOMS: SHE'D BEEN SUCKING HER THUMB AND WETTING THE BED.

MARVELLE HAAS WAS RUMORED TO BE SEEING A THERAPIST IN BAKERSFIELD. NEITHER SHE OR HER HUSBAND WERE RETURNING ANYONE'S CALLS.

"WHAT THE HELL WAS IT **ALL** FOR?" MILO HAD ASKED AFTERWARD, AS DERRICK CRIMMINS WAS BODY-BAGGED.

WEEKS LATER, I WAS **STILL** SORRY HE'D ASKED. I'D THOUGHT ABOUT LITTLE **ELSE**... HAD COME UP WITH NOTHING REAL.

FOR **FUN**? WAS IT POSSIBLE THAT CRIMMINS REALLY IMAGINED HIMSELF AS A FILMMAKER?

MILO HAD UNCOVERED NO REAL BLACK MARKET IN SNUFF FILMS, AND CRIMMINS HAD TO KNOW EVEN HOLLYWOOD WOULDN'T STOOP SO LOW. SHEER **PROFIT** AS A MOTIVE SEEMED TO BE OUT.

IN THE END, CRIMMINS SAW WHAT HE WAS DOING AS A **PRODUCTION**. HE SOMEHOW LOVED THE **PROCESS**. HE GOT HOOKED ON PLAYING GOD AFTER THE ARDULLO MASSACRE.

ARDIS PEAKE HADN'T KILLED **ANYONE**. DERRICK MURDERED THE ARDULLOS, WITH OR WITHOUT HIS BROTHER.

PEAKE WAS **NEVER** IN ANY SHAPE TO PLAN AND CONDUCT A CRIME SPREE, EVEN A SLOPPY, DISORGANIZED **MASSACRE**. HE WAS A **SCAPEGOAT**. FOR DERRICK CRIMMINS, HE WAS THE **PERFECT SURROGATE**.

DESPITE HIS CONDITION, I WAS STILL SURE PEAKE HAD **RESTRAINED** HIMSELF THAT NIGHT IN THE MOUNTAINS.

SOMETHING IN HIM FOUGHT **AGAINST** TYPE. HE REFUSED TO PLAY THE **MONSTER**.

SWIG HAD BEEN SHUFFLED INTO ANOTHER JOB, FAR AWAY FROM STARKWEATHER. PEAKE WOULD REMAIN BEHIND...**ALWAYS**.

EACH TIME I WENT, MILO ASKED IF IT WAS **WORTH** IT. WAS THERE REALLY ANYTHING IN PEAKE WORTH LISTENING TO?

"YEAH," I'D ANSWER. "IT **ALWAYS** PAYS TO LISTEN."

HELLO, ARDIS.

—THE END—

ABOUT THE AUTHOR

JONATHAN KELLERMAN is the #1 *New York Times* bestselling author of more than three dozen crime novels, including the Alex Delaware series and *The Butcher's Theater, Billy Straight, The Conspiracy Club, Twisted, True Detectives,* and *The Murderer's Daughter.* With his wife, bestselling novelist Faye Kellerman, he co-authored *Double Homicide* and *Capital Crimes.* With his son, bestselling novelist Jesse Kellerman, he co-authored *The Golem of Hollywood* and *The Golem of Paris.* He is also the author of two children's books and numerous nonfiction works, including *Savage Spawn: Reflections on Violent Children* and *With Strings Attached: The Art and Beauty of Vintage Guitars.* He has won the Goldwyn, Edgar, and Anthony awards and has been nominated for a Shamus Award. Jonathan and Faye Kellerman live in California, New Mexico, and New York.

jonathankellerman.com
Facebook.com/JonathanKellerman

About the Contributors

As an artist and writer, **ANDE PARKS** has worked for every major American comic book publisher. His writing credits include the graphic novels *Union Station* and *Capote in Kansas*. The latter was named a Notable Book for the state of Kansas in 2006, the first graphic novel to receive such an honor. His most recent graphic novel, *Ciudad*, was created with the Russo brothers (*Captain America: Civil War*) and is in development as a film project. Ande is currently writing his first prose novel. Ande lives in Kansas with his lovely wife and two children. He enjoys crime fiction, golf, vintage fedoras, and a nice glass of bourbon.

MICHAEL GAYDOS has established himself in various artistic channels. For the past twenty plus years he has worked in the world of the illustrated word and the graphic novel. His list of credits include work for Marvel, DC, Archie, Dark Circle, Boom, Virgin, Dark Horse, Random House, Fox Atomic, Image, IDW, NBC, Tundra, NBM, Caliber, and White Wolf among others. He is co-creator of Marvel's *Jessica Jones,* who currently has her own Netflix series, and has received two Eisner Award nominations for his work on *Alias* with Brian Michael Bendis. In addition to his illustration work, Michael's fine art paintings, drawings, and prints have been the subject of a number of solo exhibitions, and his art is in private collections worldwide.